Bear Island Camp

Kate Banco

Copyright

ISBN:978-17334681-8-3

DEDICATION

This book is dedicated to the children

You give us hope for the future

I also dedicate this book to my granddaughter Clara.

One day this world will be yours.

Bear Island Camp

ACKNOWLEDGMENTS

I would like to acknowledge all of my friends, family and members of the writing group Word Sisters.The year 2020 hasn't been easy on anyone. I've learned so much from the Word Sisters. I appreciate all of your guidance and friendship. This book wouldn't be finished without your help.

For that I am very grateful.

Also to my loving coffee buddies who know when to ask and when not to ask how my writing is going. Where would we be without our friends?

Last but not least, my family. We don't get to pick our families, but I have the best.

"Bear Island Camp is based on the need to provide kids with a safe place to grow and thrive. These kids weren't given a good start, the fact they were born into poverty in a country that has few opportunities for them. Their only option is to go North to work. This is troubling. You couple that with what happened to them at the border and it is a total case of family separation and most of all child abuse. We couldn't sit by and watch while that happened if we had the money and staff to help out. Bear Island Camp is the result. Now the next stage is to plan for their futures.

Our mission at Bear Camp is to rescue those who can't rescue themselves."

-Sam Mason

Fish Camp   A Young Girl's Journey to Freedom

When 17 year old Sara learns of her family's death, she accepts the role of breadwinner by crossing the US border to live with an unknown uncle. She needs to earn enough money to pay her coyote and help her Tía Elena survive. Her trip north is filled with adventure and new-found love.

Forensics Camp   Where There is Always an Unbelievable Story

No longer victims at Fish Camp, Sara and Teodoro assume the role of helpers at Forensics Camp. Sara and her husband continue their education to become crime scene investigators at SUNY Oswego in Upstate, New York

Will they take the opportunity to work in a top-secret operation to help save other young people? Their story continues as they help other young people from Mexico escape to Bear Island Camp.

The names have changed but they are the same characters. Sara and Teodoro changed their names after their latest move with WITSEC. They are now Margarita and Marcos.

Now find out the rest of the story in Bear Island Camp

Bear Island Camp

CHAPTER 1

After our first mission to rescue children from border detention camps and possibly save them from traffickers, Marcos, Dana and I get back into our morning run routine. We started running every morning at six am when we started working for Sam Mason, local humanitarian and billionaire. Our jobs with Sam help us to gain experience to reach our goal to be FBI Forensics Investigators.

The light over Lake Ontario is beautiful at six am. It is so refreshing to get the brisk air off the lake. We walk back to our apartments to shower and change. Dana, our other teammate says to have the driver pick him up at his place. We are all in a hurry to see Sam and Mary Ellen. Marilyn, the fourth teammate will already be there. It's hard not to show our pride and excitement. We finished our first mission. We rescued fifty kids from a detention center on the border.

Little did we know when we were recruited by Sam that we would be flying across country to help rescue kids. We thought we would learn more hands-on skills to help us gain knowledge about forensics. Sam says we will get more experience working for him. I agree, this first mission taught us a lot.

Our driver doesn't ask any questions about the weekend, but he knows we have been out on assignment. Everyone who works for Sam is briefed on a need-to-know basis. We decide not to discuss the weekend in the car.

As we roll up to the palatial Home Base, we see Joy's bright orange Charger parked in the lot. Other cars are lined up. I wonder to myself how many projects Sam is sponsoring. Are there other teams who help kids get to Bear Island Camp? Are there other places in the world he is helping? Before I can bring the subject up with Marcos, I see Joy walking toward us. She is dressed in her uniform of black combat pants, polo shirt and running shoes. I wonder if she ever feels like she is off duty.

"Good morning everyone, Sam is waiting for us in his office. Go and get changed, then meet us there. You ready for a debrief?"

"Yes, we all want to discuss and know more of what he has planned," Dana says.

"One operation at a time. Let's finish this one before we run off to another one, okay?" Joy says.

"We are just excited, Joy," Marcos says.

"That would be the endorphins you get from helping others. We'll get you another endorphin fix soon. In the meantime, get to Sam's office as soon as possible."

We rush from the locker room to meet up with Sam and Mary Ellen. They are seated and waiting for us. The side door opens and Marilyn walks in. I wonder how long she will continue to live here at Home Base. She must feel safer here after her kidnapping. I doubt she will ever return to live in the dorms. We were all terrified when she was kidnapped. I can't imagine how it could have been any worse for her. Sam was instrumental in her rescue.

"Well, I hear it was a successful operation," Sam says as he stands to shake each one of our hands.

"Let's go downstairs and debrief," he stands and leads us down the hall and to the stairs.

We follow him to the control room downstairs where we see all of the happenings outside the windows. Mary Ellen closes the blinds, so we won't be distracted by people and conversations outside.

"Did you complete your written evaluations?" Mary Ellen asks.

We pull out our journals and start to make excuses, "Mine isn't…."

"I almost fin…"

"Oh, I didn't think we had to turn …

Marilyn pulls out her completed journal and hands it to Sam. We all look at her and I wonder when she got it done. We spent the whole day together yesterday. Did she stay up all night to do it?

"Okay, rule number ten. Finish your evaluations within 24 hours of your return from an operation. Rule number eleven. Don't make excuses about not getting it done. You'll have some time after our meeting to work on it," Joy says.

Sheepishly, we put our unfinished journals away.

"During our de-briefings we like to be able to look at your journals and open up a discussion from what you observed and felt. We'll wing it today. But Mary Ellen and I will look at your journals before you leave, understood?" Sam isn't smiling.

"Any injuries during the operation? If so, they should have been already reported to Mary Ellen. Rule number 6."

"Do we have a list of the rules, Sam?" Marcos asks.

"No, learn them when I say them. You can help each other."

This is the first time we notice Sam in a different mood, almost like he is disappointed in us. We look at each other and decide to listen and not ask questions until he has finished.

"High points of the operation. You all returned safe, your clients all arrived at their destination safely, and you were able to return home and continue your lives without anyone finding out? Correct?" He asks without emotion.

We nod our heads in unison. None of us want to interrupt or ask questions.

"I know you all got a high from this operation. It was successful and I have to admit you all did an excellent job on your first time out. But, let me tell you, not every operation will go as smoothly as this one. We were lucky, no shots fired, no firearms used and no confrontation with the authorities at the detention center. I want to thank your leaders Joy and Mary Ellen for their smooth leadership. As always they did an excellent job."

"Let's get on to the question you all have. When is the next operation? We have some operations lined up already, but I know it's hard to balance with your school life and family. The next operation is scheduled for two weeks from now. It's a similar operation and will take all weekend."

Sam notices the look on my face and stops. "Margarita, is there a problem?"

I twist the cords on my sweatshirt nervously and I decide how much to tell Sam.

"Yes, I was hoping to talk to you alone about an issue I have," I say.

"No secrets here, Margarita. If it affects you it affects your team. Go ahead, what is your concern?" Sam asks.

"Well, you see if Marcos and I need to be gone on operations a lot, it will get more difficult to hide our work from my family. I hate to lie to them. This weekend worked but I'm not sure how to handle the other operations. Do you have any thoughts or ideas?" I ask.

"Of course, we do. But, you are always one jump ahead of us Margarita," Mary Ellen says and smiles.

"We looked at your school calendar and see Spring Break is coming up. We have one operation between now and then. We want to wait until Spring Break to reveal our ideas you can share with your families. Can you wait for that?" Sam asks.

"Yes, if we have a good cover story for the next operation. I can wait until Spring Break for the other trips," I say.

"Sam, I have similar issues because I work with Margarita's parents. I know I'll need to quit that job soon, but they depend on me. I also need a good story," Dana says.

"We will brief you soon, we need to finish this operation first. You will be briefed on the next operation on Friday," Sam answers.

"Okay some quick questions. How difficult did you find working with the children? On a scale of 1-10 how difficult were they to work with? I'll ask you individually."

"Margarita, go," Sam says.

"One is least difficult? Then one."

"Dana?"

"Same, a one"

"Marcos?"

"I agree, they were very easy to work with, a one."

Marilyn says, "I agree with them."

"Okay, next question I only want a score, no comments. How difficult was it to work with Joy and Mary Ellen as your leaders?"

We all answer the same answer, one.

"How difficult was it for you to leave the children on Bear Island? Go!"

Marcos answers first, "Ten."

I echo his answer. "Ten."

Marilyn says, "Eleven."

Dana laughs and says, "Ten."

"Okay, so you all made a connection with the kids?" Sam asks.

We all nod our heads yes in unison.

"If you told me our next operation is to go back to Bear Island and spend time with those kids I'd say absolutely. I'm ready to go," Dana smiles.

Marilyn agrees, "Me too, they are fantastic kids."

"No comments from you two?" Sam asks.

"We agree, we've talked about it," Marcos says.

"Good because your next operation is for you to return to Bear Island Camp. We'll brief you on Friday. It won't be for two weeks, but that is a stopover for you. You'll get to see some of the kids then."

"Stopover? Where will we end up?" Marcos asks.

"Friday, you will get the details. Now, I need you to go finish those journals and work with Joy. You have some gear to unpack. We'll see you before you leave today. Great job, just get those journals to me today."

At this point Sam stands up and indicates it's time for us to leave and go finish our work. We walk back upstairs with Joy. She sends us out of the office to the computer lab to work on our journals and says, "Make sure you get them done."

We grab our backpacks and walk outside. We head to the computer lab area where we can sit comfortably and finish our work. Marilyn comes with us to make some more notes on her already completed journal.

On the walk to the computer lab I say, "Where do you think we'll go on our next flight? Sam said we will return to Bear Island, but he also said it won't be our final destination. Do you guys have any idea where we might go? Do you think it will be dangerous?"

Memories of my previous panic attacks come to mind. I break out into a sweat. No one notices and I walk ahead to reach the computer room first.

Dana answers first, "No clue, I have no idea. I'm glad we are returning to see the kids, but I wonder what else this trip will include. Sam doesn't give very many hints, does he?"

"I think you need to give Sam the benefit of the doubt. He won't put us in harm's way. It will be a safe operation I'm sure," Marilyn says.

Marilyn has known Sam for a much longer time than we have. Her statement calms me a little bit. I don't want to have a panic attack now. I don't want the others to see me like that. Marcos may notice and knows what to do. Marilyn and Dana have never seen me have a panic attack.

"What if we have to transport some of the kids to a new destination or to a hospital. Memo is still very sick. That could be it. But I do worry about what we are going to tell your parents. I don't like making up stories. They will start to figure out something strange is going on," Marcos says.

"I know, I hate the thought of lying to my parents again, but I am also excited to go. I really liked meeting the kids and helping them out. Do you think that's what Sam wants us to write in our journals? Our concerns and worries?" I ask.

"Write how you felt, if you felt safe or if you were afraid. Tell him what you felt when you first saw the kids in the cages sleeping on the floor. Write about how hard it was to leave them on Bear Island. It's so far away from their families. They have to be scared. Write it all," Marilyn says. "That's what I did."

"I can write so much about my feelings, I guess that is what a journal is for, isn't it? Let's get it done so we can give them to Sam. I think he is eager to read what we thought about the operation. He has a lot at stake here and he wants to know if he can depend on us or not. If we get all emotional on our first time out, he may reconsider sending us again. I think it's okay to write about your feelings, but I also think it's important to say how we were able to come back home and get back to normal life. Part of this is fitting back in. No one knows where we were or what we did. So, it has to be because we are invested in the operations. I think it's important to let him know that," Dana says.

We use our ID cards to enter the computer lab and I'm happy to see the independent work area with sofas and easy chairs is completely empty. We rush over to claim our spaces and get to work.

One hour passes by without any of us saying a word. We are so intent on getting our work done. Marilyn is the first one to stand up to stretch her legs. She walks over to the water cooler and pours four cups of water. She brings them back and sets one in front of each of us.

"Okay guys, time to get up and move. We've all written a novel in our journals. Let's move on to something else," Marilyn says.

We finish our last sentences and close our journals. I think next time I'll start my journal on the plane home. It will save a lot of time. We walk together back to Sam's office. As we enter Sam asks us to all sit down. We thought we would just drop our journals off and leave.

"Something has come up and we need to schedule another flight for this weekend," Sam says.

My stomach does a flip flop and I start to feel nauseous, beads of sweat form on my forehead. I feel a panic attack coming on. Marcos looks over at me and grabs my hand.

"Breathe," he whispers to me.

"Don't worry, we have come up with a solution for your family. If you trust me, I think we can make the problem go away," Sam says.

"What? That scares me Sam. Are you talking about my family as a problem?"

Sam holds his hand up and tells me to stop.

"Margarita, don't put words in my mouth. I didn't say that. I said we have found a solution for the problem of lying to your parents. Give me a day or two and things will start to make sense. In the meantime, prepare to leave Friday afternoon. You will be back in town Sunday night, late. Any questions?"

Marcos raises his hand and says, "I have a question Sam. Will we get a schedule or know more in advance when operations are? We have our classes and studies. I think out stress will increase if we don't know what to expect."

"Good question, Marcos. I may as well tell you now, what we are working on. Sit down all of you." Sam says.

Mary Ellen looks over at Sam and nods her head in agreement before saying, "Sam is working very hard to stay ahead of your questions."

I feel bad if we are too aggressive, but I also don't want to be involved in any activities I'm not sure about. What if he sends us somewhere and asks us to do something we aren't comfortable with?

Sam clears his throat and pulls out a packet from his top desk drawer. "I can't share all of the particulars Margarita, but I can share with you that your parent's taco shop is almost sold."

"What? I don't understand. My parents wouldn't do that before discussing it with Marcos and me. It's impossible. Why do you think this?" I say in a raised voice.

Sam opens the packet and shows a copy of the agreement between my Papá and Mamá. "Here, it is. They are in the process of signing right now. My real estate agent is there now with an offer they can't refuse. It will pay off their debt and give them enough money to do whatever they want. Mary Ellen and I have been working on this for some time. We knew you would need a more permanent solution."

"I can't believe it. How could they do that without talking with me first?" I cry. My shortness of breath returns and beads of sweat form on my forehead.

"They do have 24 hours to cancel the contract. They can change their mind. They haven't received any money yet except for the down payment."

At that moment my phone buzzes in my pocket. I don't want to be rude to Sam and Mary Ellen, but I am curious to see if the call is from my parents. Sam indicates to me with a nod and gestures to me to answer the phone.

As I pull out the phone, I can see it is from Mamá. I stand up and walk away from the others to have some privacy.

"Hija, we need to come over tonight to talk to you. Or can you stop by the taquería? No, no te preocupes hija. It's good news, very good news. Don't worry!" She says.

"So, everyone is okay?" I ask.

"Yes, todos bien!" She says.

"Why don't you come over tonight and I'll cook dinner. You sound very excited. Come about 6 o'clock."

"Okay, we'll be there. ¡Hasta entonces!

"Bye, Mamá," I say as I turn to see everyone waiting to hear what Mamá said.

"It's must be true what you said, it sounds like they are very excited. It must be about the sale, right?" I say.

Sam starts to speak, and Marcos interrupts him, "Sam, we signed up to work for you, not our family. This makes me feel a little uneasy. It feels like we don't have control of anything."

Sam smiles and says, "You asked for a solution and I found one. I don't do this for everyone, but this group is all connected to this family. By purchasing the taco shop it solves a lot of issues you have."

"I don't understand how," I say.

Mary Ellen indicates to us to let Sam tell us his whole plan. I'm very uneasy and I can see Dana and Marcos are too. Marilyn doesn't look as concerned but because she knows Sam better than we do. Sam pulls out four more packets. He shows them to us; they are recruitment packs like the ones Joy had us sign.

"I don't understand, these are recruitment forms," I say again.

"Think about what our long-term plans are. Maybe you aren't aware of the plans for Bear Island Camp but believe me once the four of you started working we decided to pull in the rest of your family in. We want you to all work with us. These recruitment packets are for your family," Sam says and stands up.

"Go home now, do what you normally do on a Tuesday, have dinner with your family. Find out their reaction to the sale. Tomorrow it will all make sense to you. No more questions and remember don't tell your parents you are aware of the sale. Let them surprise you!"

We stand up and I feel frustrated that we can't get the whole story now. Sam smiles and says, "I wouldn't do anything to hurt you or your parents. Please remember that. We spend a lot of time and money in our recruitment and training. We take care of our workers. Keep that in mind. See you tomorrow."

Joy waits for us outside Sam's door and says, "Trust Sam, it will all work out. Believe me. I can't share what he has planned, but I know you will be happy with the plans. Everyone will be happy."

I start to ask a question, "Joy" but she cuts me off and says, "No more questions Margarita, not today. Go home, talk it over with Marcos, Dana and Marilyn. Tomorrow is another day."

On the drive home we are quiet because no one knows what to expect. What will my parents do without the taco shop? What will Sandy and Junior do? Will they make enough money from the sale to live comfortably? My Papá is getting older, it will be hard for him to work for someone else. I think they planned on Sandy and Junior taking over the taco shop. Now what?

Marcos is the first to say anything out loud, "Have you thought that maybe Sam will pay enough money for your parents to retire? It's a possibility."

"They love their work; they love working with students and customers from the community. They are very social, they like working with the public," I say.

"Let's see what they say tonight. How about we all go for coffee?" Marcos says.

Marilyn says, "Yes, let's go to Dunkin Donuts. I'm hungry!"

We all laugh because Marilyn has said very little all day, but now she seems very excited to go for coffee and donuts. Our mood changes and we all relax a little.

CHAPTER 2

My family come over as they said they would, and with them a cloud of excitement comes through the door. Sandy and Junior can't wait to tell us what the news is. Mamá is smiling and runs over to give me a hug. Papá looks so excited. I can't help but notice how grown up Sandy looks; she is still young but she looks like she could be a college student. When did that happen?

"You aren't going to believe what has happened, hija," my Papá says.

"Let's sit down and you can tell us. Marcos has hamburgers and a salad ready. Sit down next to me and tell me what is so exciting," I say.

"You'll never believe it! Someone wants to buy the taqueria and for a lot of money. There's no way we can say no. The offer is so generous." Papá says.

"That's not all, Margarita," Sandy says.

"Wait, one thing at a time. First, who wants to buy the taco shop? Were you thinking of selling it?" Marcos asks.

"Okay, I'll tell the story. Two days ago, a young well-dressed lady came into the taqueria. She ordered some food, then asked if we were interested in advertising the business for sale. I told her no, we have no plans to sell it. We are happy with our business. She left her card and said to call her if we changed our minds. The next day she came back, ordered food again and asked the same question. I laughed and said no, we aren't interested. She thanked us and said she would be back again."

Mamá laughs and says, "We thought it was so unusual to have someone so interested in our business."

"Hurry, tell them the next part," Junior says.

"Okay, yesterday the same lady came back, but this time with a briefcase and another man. She introduced us and said the man has a check for us, wants to put a down payment on the taco shop and wants to purchase the business by the end of the month."

"Wait, they gave you money already? Did you sign anything, Papá?" I ask. I can feel the bile rising in my throat. This is so scary. I don't want to lie to my parents but I act like I don't know.

"Only that I received ten thousand dollars as a down payment. If the sale doesn't go through, we get to keep the down payment," he says.

"Did you accept it? Is that normal?" Marcos asks.

"We don't know, Marcos. All we know is that we have a week to change our minds. We wanted to talk to you first. We don't want to make any mistakes," Papá says as he looks me in the eyes.

"Can we see the paperwork?" I ask.

"Sure, here it is."

The name of the buyer is on the paper. I think it's someone who already owns a lot of the downtown area.

I look over at Marcos to see what he is thinking. He signals to me to go to the kitchen.

"I need to get some water, anyone else?" I ask.

"No gracias, hija," Mamá answers.

"I'll help you," Marcos says as he follows me into the kitchen.

"Is this what Sam means by a solution? He did buy the taco shop."

"I'm not sure Margarita, but one thing for sure Sam doesn't let things get in the way if he can solve them with money. He pays our tuition, he flies us around to help other people, he buys the taco shop because he thinks it was an issue for us. I wonder what his next step is? He must have a plan," Marcos says.

We walk back to the living room and Sandy is telling my papá something and encouraging him to finish the story.

"There's more Margarita. Papá has more news," Sandy says with excitement.

"What else could happen? I say.

"Well, the same lady who brought us the check and sold the taco shop put up a sign in the window that says SOLD. It is quite a shock to see that sign in our window. We didn't plan on any of this."

"And? What is the other news?" I ask.

"Right after the sign went up in the window our customers started asking us why we were selling and who would buy the business. They all seemed disappointed to see us go. Then a man we've never met before came in. He had some brochures of a beautiful place. He said they are looking for a husband and wife to run their kitchen at a camp for children. The only question I have is how did he just happen to stop in? And the camp is in Canada. I'm not sure we can go. Do we need to check with WITSEC to leave the country? How will we get permission to work in

Canada?" Papá sighs and it looks like his excitement has turned to worry.

"And you, Marcos, Yasmene, Miguel and the children won't be there. I don't think we want to go that far away from you. But Sandy and Junior are all excited after looking at the brochures. They would give us a log cabin to live in, the whole family is invited, and Sandy and Junior can participate in the camp activities for free. That idea excites them."

What if the camp is too much work?" I ask.

"No, it is less work. We would be responsible for the kitchen and we would work five days a week. No more weekends. One meal a day is served buffet style. We will have assistants and lots of helpers. The children will be in a healthy environment. It looks so beautiful. Did I tell you it's on an island?" Papá smiles.

I look at Marcos and decide to congratulate them on their announcements. "It sounds wonderful, would Sandy and Junior go to school there too? Or is it only for the summer?" I ask.

"They told us they would give us more details. We have an interview next week. We can decide not to go. We do like living here in Oswego, but it sounds like so much fun," Mamá says.

"We would like you to come with us, do you think that's possible?" Mamá asks.

"Well, they did say there is room for the whole family, didn't they? I'm sure we can visit," I say.

Everyone stays a little while longer and we talk about what fun it would be to live on an island again. We enjoyed living on Orcas Island. The water in the Puget Sound had very relaxing qualities. Little do they know, this time it will so different, it will be an island on the

26

Atlantic Ocean and much farther north. The winters will be cold, but the summers should be very enjoyable. But more than that they will be working for Sam and they will become part of our team. Sam does seem to have a solution for everything.

Bear Island Camp

CHAPTER 3

The next day Marcos and I are eager to get to Home Base. We both had problems sleeping after learning of Sam's plan. I need to speak to him. I have so many questions.

We leave campus after our run. Both of us are quiet as our driver takes us to Home Base. When we arrive at the house we are ushered right into Sam's office.

"Good morning, you two. I suppose you have a lot of questions for me. Please take a seat," Sam says as he also sits down behind his desk.

"Good morning," we both say in unison.

"First, let me explain before you start with your questions. Maybe I will have an answer and you won't have to ask so many questions," Sam says.

At this point Mary Ellen walks into Sam's office and greets us all. She has a very serious look on her face, and I wonder if something has happened.

"Ok, there was a very generous offer on your parent's taco shop. They seem interested but haven't signed any papers yet. They said they wanted to talk it over with you."

Sam hesitates before continuing and I say, "We understand you are trying to keep us together with my family. But it seems like a lot to ask of them to leave their business, other family members and schools."

"Like I said, they received a very generous offer. More than what the business is worth. You didn't let me finish. They also received a generous job offer as well. They interview next week but if they choose to work with us the job is theirs for as long as they want. The package we offer will include employment, housing, schools, insurance and a beautiful place to raise their family. Our goal is to grow the community on Bear Island Camp. Your parents will be one of the first families we hire as full-time staff."

"That sounds almost too perfect, I feel like we should be asking you a million questions. Is there a catch?" Marcos asks.

"Has there been a catch in anything we've told you since we hired you? We have always been very upfront about everything," Mary Ellen says with an edge to her voice.

"No, but this is my family. I worry about them. What if it's not a place they want to live? What if they arrive and Sandy or Junior don't like it? Can they leave or quit?" I ask.

"Of course, we have always said that you are free to leave. But since you signed a non-disclosure agreement you won't be able to tell anyone about Bear Island Camp or any of our operations. Do you think there is any reason they wouldn't like it?" Sam asks.

"No, I just worry about Sandy and Junior. They have had to move so much, and they are so young," I sigh.

"Margarita, what about everything you went through on your trip from Baja? You traveled alone and risked your safety. You were aboard a ship with people you had never met. How did it turn out for you? Do you feel in danger now?" Sam questions me with an almost angry look.

"Sam, no. I don't feel in danger. I just want to be cautious. I survived because I was cautious and also because I had people watching out for me. It was scary but I don't feel in danger now. But we are always on the lookout for situations that could be dangerous. My Tío Enrique has many friends and what if they found us? We still need to be careful," I explain. I flash back to the time I spent with Tío Enrique and his family. He told me he would sell me to traffickers if I came forward with the information I had about him. It was a very scary time.

Marcos jumps in and says, "Sam, we are very thankful for everything you have done for us. We worry about other people, not you. We trust you totally."

Mary Ellen's face relaxes when Marcos says this.

"Sam, we don't doubt you ever. We know how much you do to help people. I'm thankful you are helping my family. Please don't get angry. I don't want them to be surprised by a situation that might be too much for them."

Sam smiles and says, "Okay, I think we are now on the same page. Are you okay with what we have offered your family? Are you okay with them moving to Bear Island Camp and working for us?"

I look at Marcos and answer for both of us, "Yes we are okay with it. How will you explain to them about what we do?"

"That will all be explained in the interview. First you will come with them and explain on the way where they are going. Joy will ride with you. We'll send a van and pick you two up first, then your parents. They agreed you could come with them on the interview, right?"

"Yes, I told them we both want to be there for the interview," I say and nod my head.

"Okay, so on Monday morning the interview will be here at nine in the morning. Your brother and sister will go to school as usual. We don't need to involve them until your parents have accepted employment. Okay I can see you already have another question. Go ahead," Sam smiles.

"Well, you know we have more family. Yasmene and Miguel and they have two children. How do we explain to them that we are all moving away and leaving them here in Oswego? I don't know what to tell them. They will be very sad and probably won't understand."

Mary Ellen speaks up and says what Joy usually tells me, "Margarita you are always asking about the next problem before we've solved the first one. You are jumping ahead of us. We also have plans for them."

"What, what kind of plans? They are both still studying and won't finish for at least two years. I don't think they will want to give up their studies."

"Do you want to know everything we have planned for the next year, Margarita?" Sam says sarcastically but with a smile.

"Sorry, I need my family all together. When we left the ship, we all agreed we would stick together. I would feel like we've abandoned them."

"Mary Ellen, could you get Juan to bring in some coffee and pastries? I have a feeling this meeting will go on for longer than expected and I need coffee to stay ahead of Margarita," Sam throws a folder to the side of the desk and opens a drawer.

We wait while Mary Ellen asks Juan to bring us our coffees. I can see that Marcos is worried about getting back to class. But this is too important. I whisper to him, "We need to get everything clear before we bring my parents into this. I know they won't want to leave part of the family behind."

Marcos nods his head in agreement and relaxes a little.

By the time Juan has brought in a tray of coffees and croissants, Sam has moved us over to a conference table. Before us he has spread out some blueprints of Bear Island Camp. We never got to see the whole island, we only toured the small area surrounding the lodge, the cabins where we stayed and the medical center. We didn't have free time to see the rest of the island.

We each grab our mugs of coffee and I'm grateful the coffee is hot and delicious. The croissants are also very fresh. If this wasn't an important meeting about our future I would relax and enjoy the coffee.

Sam sips from his coffee mug and says, "We had no plan to show you our next phase of Bear Island Camp. It was going to be on a need to know basis. Since you both want to be prepared, we may as well fill you in our long-term plan."

"The next trip you go on will be to transport some of the kids back to their parents. Some of the parents are American citizens and were detained in the group by mistake. We have been able to contact families who live in the United States, work and have made homes there. They have legal rights to their children. We will make that happen and get them back to their homes next weekend. It's not our fault they were mixed in with the rescue operation, but they did need rescuing. We have the ability to make the contacts, check the paperwork and get those kids home. Our intention was not to take kids from their families."

"What about the ones whose parents were deported or detained? What will happen to them?" I ask.

"That is the next phase of Bear Island Camp. We have a long-term goal to bring carefully selected families to live on Bear Island Camp. The kids from the detention camps will have the option of living with a family. We feel it is the best therapy for those kids, find a family who will love them and keep them stable. If we find their families, they can choose to return or stay."

"Do you mean they wouldn't return to their families even though they have been found?" Marcos asks.

"Yes, we are drafting a protocol to use with each situation. We can talk more about that later. We haven't finalized the plans yet. We have built cabins for each family. One of those cabins is where your family will live. It will be a community with churches, schools and sports fields."

"It sounds like a type of idealistic society," Marcos says.

Mary Ellen and Sam both smile. Mary Ellen says, "Do you mean where children live with loving families, have healthcare, good schools and lots of places to play? If that is your definition of idealistic, then that is what it is. We are trying to save kids."

"What about bringing the families to them? Rescue the families from detention centers and bring them here," I ask.

"That is a possibility, but right now we are focusing on reuniting the families in their homes and creating new homes for the kids whose families we can't find. We have to take baby steps; right now our goal is to help those kids who are alone," Sam explains.

"You said you have a solution for Yasmene and Miguel. Where do they fit?" I ask.

"Patience is not one of your strong suits, is it?" Sam says as he looks at me. "Our plan is to offer them a similar package of employment. We need teachers and Miguel is studying to be a teacher, right? We need nurses and doctors. I believe Yasmene is studying nursing, is that right?"

"Yes, Miguel wants to teach and Yasmene wants to be a nurse."

Mary Ellen smiles and says, "They are perfect recruits for Bear Island Camp. We need them and if they accept, your whole family will be there in one place. It may not be right away but when you finish your studies."

The smile on my face disappears and Sam looks at me and says, "What now?"

Marcos and I look at each other. I'm sure he knows what I'm thinking.

"We are thankful for everything you are doing but our hope is to one day work for the FBI."

Sam laughs, then Mary Ellen laughs too.

"It's true your training here will help you walk right into an FBI agent position. But let me ask you a question. Do you think you'll have more power or importance there? Look, you haven't even finished college and you already participated in a covert rescue operation to help save fifty kids. Your days as an FBI agent will be boring compared to what we have planned for you two. You can keep your goal and still dream about it, but I guarantee you if you stay with us you will get much more self-satisfaction than hunting down criminals for the FBI."

"If you apply to the FBI and get accepted you will have the option of leaving us. I hope you don't, but we can't hold you here. Please give us three years, then you can make a choice. By then you will finish your studies and be able to make an educated decision. Keep your goals! Without goals, where would any of us be? I'd like you both to think about one thing though. What if your goal were to be a group leader or director of operations here one day? This organization will continue long after Mary Ellen and I are gone. We'll need some intelligent and inquisitive agents to take over. Think about it," Sam says as he stands up and indicates the meeting is over.

Marcos and I are overwhelmed with all of the information we learned today. Did Sam just offer us a higher-level position when we finish our studies? Did he really say director of operations?

Before we leave, I turn and ask one more question, "Sam, what is the timeline for the whole family to move to Bear Island Camp?"

Sam laughs and says, "You are always in such a hurry. Patience, patience. First, we will get your parents on board, then the following week we will call in the other two. When your parents come to the interview, we will let them know that we plan to relocate Yasmene and Miguel also. I'm sure it will be a question they have. We chose your family because you are so tight knit, and you've all been through so much together. You also have the capability of keeping secrets. You've all demonstrated that. Did I mention yours is the perfect family? Don't worry so much Margarita. We'll take care of everyone."

CHAPTER 4

The day of the interview, a driver picks Marcos and I up at our apartment. He has been instructed to get us in the car before he picks up my parents. They will be more at ease if we are in the car. Joy accompanies us to help get NDAs signed.

On the drive to the taquería Marcos looks over at me and says, "You are worried, aren't you?"

"Yes, of course. I know we did the right thing working with Sam and Mary Ellen, but I'm not sure what Sam will ask my parents to do. It worries me."

"We'll find out soon enough. Look, we are almost downtown, and I can see your parents are out front waiting. I'm so glad Dana and Marilyn could help out today so they can go to the interview," Marcos smiles. "Good thing we have best friends, right?"

"Yes, I agree. Dana and Marilyn are life savers. We need friends like them," I say.

The driver pulls up in front of the taqueria and Marcos jumps out to open the door for my parents.

"Right this way, señores. Your limo awaits you!" Marcos says jokingly.

"Oh my, such a nice car to take us to the interview," Mamá giggles.

Joy introduces herself and then sits back to let me handle everything.

They start to relax, and I see they are both smiling. I hope their smiles last all day. What if they decide not to accept Sam's job offer?

"Mamá and Papá, I have some papers for you to sign before we get to the interview," I say cautiously.

"What kind of papers? For the sale of the restaurant? What papers?" My dad asks.

"Qué pasa, hija? You have me worried now. What is this?" Mamá asks.

"The man who offered you a job is called Sam Mason; we also work for him. We were asked to keep it a secret. It is like undercover work you see on TV shows. We work for him and he pays our tuition and some extra."

"What? You both have money for tuition from the money you got from WITSEC and the sale of the Mexican Restaurant on Orcas Island. Is that money gone?" My dad asks.

"No, we have enough money, it is part of the deal. Marilyn and Dana also work for him. He helped find Marilyn when she was kidnapped. He has been helping her for a long time."

"I don't understand. Who is this Sam Mason?" My dad asks.

Marcos jumps in with some much-needed comments about our situation, "He's a wealthy man who helps people. We can share more after you sign the paperwork. What it says is that after the interview if you decide to not accept the work you will keep anything he said to you a secret. No one can know. That's what this signature means. It means you understand what you are about to hear is top secret."

"Margarita, is this safe?" Mamá asks.

"Yes, it is safe, and he helps a lot of people. But you can decide whether or not to join us. I believe his plan to hire you is so we can all be together. If you go to Bear Island Camp to work, we will also be there all summer and coming back here in the fall to finish school. Once we finish school, we will be full time on Bear Island Camp. At least that is what he explained to us yesterday."

"We'll sign the papers, but we want to be able to say no if anything feels dangerous. Do you understand?" Papá says as he signs the document and hands the pen to Mamá. "It worries me because we just want a quiet life near our kids and grandkids. What about Yasmene and Miguel? Will they stay here?"

"Sam assured us yesterday he will offer them employment next week if you decide to work for him. He says he wants us all together if that means it's the best for us. We told him we couldn't move to Bear Island Camp unless our family was there. He is doing this to keep us all together," I say.

"Okay, I trust you, but I may not trust Sam Mason. Where are we going?" My dad asks as he looks at the boats on Lake Ontario.

"Home Base, where we work, is outside of town in a hidden place. It's hard to find if you don't know where it is. It's on the lake and beautiful," Marcos says with a twinkle in his eye. I can see he is happier now with the thought of my parents joining forces with us. I forget how much they mean to him. He lost both parents at an early age and had to fend for himself most of his life. When we married, my family became his family.

The driver pulls up to the guard booth. Marcos and I show our badges. We also give my parents' names and say Sam is waiting to speak to them. He calls the house as always to check. He waves us through after closing his phone.

"Why so much security?" Papá asks.

"You'll see once you meet Sam. He will explain everything, and we'll be there with you the whole time. I'm so glad Sam wants you to work for him," I say.

When we pull up in front of Sam's house, I hear Mamá let out a sigh of relief. Maybe she thought we were taking her to some military-like building. I'm glad she is relieved now.

When Juan opens the door and greets us, he calls my parents by name. "Welcome Francesca and Luis. Follow me, Sam is waiting for you in his office."

My parents look like they can't believe Juan knew their names.

"He would make a very good businessman," Papá says. "It's always good to call people by their names."

We are ushered into Sam's office and Mary Ellen stands to greet us. Sam enters from a side door and rushes to shake hands with my parents.

"Welcome, I'm happy you decided to come today. I hope you will feel welcome here. Have a seat and we can get started," he smiles.

"Did you bring the papers?" he asks me.

"Yes." I hand the signed papers over and he does the same thing he did the first day I arrived here with Joy. He opens a drawer of his desk and files them.

"You must have so many questions. I want to start by saying your daughter and son-in-law are great workers and we have enjoyed getting to know them. I'm sure you all will have lots to talk about after our interview. First, if I may, I'd like to tell you what the offer is. When I finish, you can ask any questions you want. Sound fair?"

My parents both nod their heads in agreement. They look over at me to see if I look scared or worried. Since I show no signs of fear they seem to relax.

"Well, Mary Ellen and I work here and have projects we help with. One of our goals is to help people who are in trouble. We recruit people who we think can help us with this task. That's why we want to offer you two employment. We don't call it a job because it is more than a job, it is an invitation to join a lifestyle and be a crucial part of building a great community. Don't worry, we aren't recruiting you for a religious mission or to become members of a church or cult. You don't have to worry about that."

Sam pauses and looks at us to see if things are going well.

"We have purchased Bear Island; it is an island off the coast of Nova Scotia. It is part of Canada. We are building a community there and need your help. We have rescued some children. All ages, from babies to teenagers. We need families to move there, live and become part of the community. People like yourselves who have older children, can offer some work but most importantly help the children who don't have parents."

I start to fidget in my chair and Sam knows I have a question.

"I see Margarita is concerned so I'm going to let her ask one question. Margarita, go," he says.

"Are you asking my parents to be foster parents? I'm not sure if they will want to do that."

"No, absolutely not. If they choose to reach out to kids that is their option. We want to hire them because of their restaurant experience and cooking skills. We need a manager and assistant to run our food services. It is a thought that you, Francesca and Luis, might be interested. Don't answer yet, I haven't given you any details."

I try to look at them to see what they might feel, and there is no way of telling. They look stunned and I worry it might be too much for them.

"Let me continue. We are in the process of building a new school and hiring teachers. Your kids will be offered top-notch education from fantastic teachers. The classes may be small at first, but we expect to have a full K-12 program within the year. We have already started classes in our community building until the school is finished. We also have a staffed medical center if you need a doctor or dentist, completely free to island residents. Your housing is also free. I have set aside one of our newer cabins for you. There is room for you and your two children who live at home, and there is an extra room if you have visitors."

"You might be worried about a paycheck or expenses you may have. You will both receive a paycheck deposited into a bank account monthly. Retirement will also be paid into a separate account. Your kids will have opportunities to attend universities when they are ready, but we can talk about that later. Questions?"

I see my dad hesitate, look down and form the question before he speaks, "What is the work? You want us to cook? Manage the food service? I know we can do that and the benefits you offer are very generous. But, my question is, why are you offering it to us? Why us?"

"Very good question. First your experience, second you are Margarita's parents. I know if you stay here, I'll never be able to get Marcos and Margarita to move to Bear Island Camp. They are an important part of our project. We need someone to manage food service and your daughter needs you to be nearby. I also know your background and what you both have been through. I want to make things easier for you all. You have had some terrible experiences."

Papá gives me a worried look and says, "Margarita, how much does he know?"

"They know everything, but we haven't shared anything with them. They have connections with WITSEC. We never would have risked our safety before checking with WITSEC. This isn't a bad thing. We will be finishing school, you and Mamá are getting older. You may not want to work as much. This is a solution, Papá."

"The position we are offering is Managers of Food Service. You will coordinate and manage; it doesn't mean you need to work twelve hours a day cooking. You will have assistants and helpers. You will be in charge and supervise others," Sam says.

Mamá speaks up, "My husband gets tired easily now. It is a relief to sell the taqueria. I worry it will be too much for him, for both of us. We are tired."

"We want someone who knows how to run a kitchen, how to offer good food and make sure it is available when needed. You will have the option of working early or working late. You won't work breakfast and dinner. It probably will be either breakfast and lunch, or lunch and dinner. We have very good help there now. It's just a matter of making it better. A large majority of the residents are from Mexico, at least for now. They will enjoy your home cooked food I'm sure. You can make a variety of food, but we also want someone who makes the best Mexican food. I hear that is you Francesca," Sam says with a smile.

Wow, he knows what to say to Mamá. Give her a compliment on her cooking and she'll sign up right now. But, she'll wait for Papá's agreement before answering. "You are very kind," she says.

"Another question I have. We have Yasmene and Miguel and our two grandchildren. We won't want to be far away from them. I'm not sure what to do. We solve one problem but there is another one," Papá says sadly.

"We have a solution for them too. Remember I said we have a school and a medical center? They will be offered work next week if you decide to join us. I don't want to make them an offer until you decide if it works for you. Does that sound fair?"

"Yes, that sounds fair. If we decide to go when would we start?" Papá asks.

Marcos looks at me and smiles. He knows my dad has made his decision but won't commit to it until he's talked with us.

"Very good question. I have to let you know that Marcos and Margarita will be going on some weekend trips. This won't have an effect on you except that now you will know why they are gone for long weekends."

Mamá looks over at me with a smile, "Niagara Falls? Was that a long-weekend trip?"

"Yes, I'll explain later. We had to tell you a story. It was our first trip and we had no idea how to leave for a long weekend without telling you top-secret information."

"We will set up a visit so you can fly out to see your home and work area. Will that help you make a decision? Once you talk with your younger children and you let them know they can't tell anyone. We ask they only say they are moving. They will be able to contact friends after the move, but not specific details. I hope that is okay, it has to be that way."

"No problem, they have been in WITSEC and know as long as we are together, they can't share details. We were split up from Margarita and we don't want that to happen again. We'll speak to them," Mamá says.

"Luis and Francesca, if you are thinking of joining us, I can get started on your ID badges and your health checkup," Mary Ellen says.

"Medical? Why?" Papá asks.

"We want our partners to be healthy. You won't be excluded if you have an illness, but we want to know so we can get you the best care. Does that sound okay?" Mary Ellen stands.

Papá and Mamá look over at the two of us, "Should we join you? What if Sandy and Junior don't like it there?"

Sam looks over and answers, "We will have soccer teams, art classes, dance classes and a movie night every week. We have an activity director who will help your kids find what they like. The atmosphere on the island is very relaxed and less stressful. Only traffic is construction vehicles and a few golf carts. Bicycles and swimming in the summer. I have a feeling they might like it. Since your kids are bilingual, they will fit right into the bilingual school. I'm sure they will excel; some of the other students will be behind. We will have whatever they need for school. You ask what happens if they don't like it. We don't like to think of our partners leaving, but as a family if it didn't work out, we could come up with a solution. "

"Do you want to join us?" Sam asks.

I see my dad reach over and grab Mamá's hand. "¿Qué piensas? ¿Vamos a la isla?"

"Yes, I think we should do this. Let's try it," Mamá answers.

Sam stands up to shake their hands and say welcome!

Marcos and I rush over to hug them both. "You have no idea how much easier this will be if you are there too. I think you'll love it there. The kids need us, and they need you. I think you will love them!"

Mary Ellen says, "Let's get your badge and a quick medical check. Follow me, please. Do you need Margarita to join you?"

"No, I think if we go together, we'll be fine," Mamá says.

I watch them go next door with Mary Ellen. I'm relieved they are agreeable so far.

Sam tells us to sit down. "This weekend we will have your second mission. Tomorrow when Dana, Marilyn and you both are here, Joy will brief you on what the mission is. It will include a lot of flying, so bring comfortable clothes for the flight home and you might be able to sleep. It's a round trip including a few layovers. I'll give you the details tomorrow. Any questions?"

"No, Sam. Thank you for finding a solution for our family. I will be more focused if I don't have to lie to my parents."

"That is what I need to hear, we have some complicated missions coming up and we need your head in the game. You and Marcos will be an important part of the team missions coming up because of your Spanish. This next one might be difficult. Get some rest, I'll fill you in tomorrow."

Bear Island Camp

CHAPTER 5

My parents are so excited on the ride back into town. The questions keep coming and each time the word island seems to be what excites them the most. Maybe they have great memories of when we first lived on Orcas Island. It was an incredible experience. We were happy there. I thought they were happy here working in the taqueria, but maybe they longed to go back to Orcas Island where we were first placed when we joined WITSEC.

We drop them off and Marcos and I asked to be dropped off on campus. So much has happened this week. First, the taqueria was sold then my parents agreed to work with Sam and move to Bear Island Camp. Life is moving so fast for us. Tomorrow, we'll find out what our mission is for this weekend. I am excited but fearful at the same time. The rest of the day seems like a blur.

The next day comes too early and we are tired. Marcos is deep in thought while we get ready the following day to go to Home Base. It's a normal workday for us, yet we realize now that our family is involved it is even more important that we are on top of things. We don't want anything to happen to them.

Dana is already in the car when we walk outside. He is unaware of the news; we haven't told him or Marilyn yet.

"Hey Dana, my parents asked me if you can work this weekend." I say with a serious look on my face.

"What? I can't! We need to come up with a story," he says with a frown on his face.

Marcos and I both start to laugh. Dana looks at us with an angry look.

"What are you up to? It's not funny. You know how hard it is for me to say no to your parents. I can't believe you two."

"Dana, it's a joke. You don't have to worry anymore. The taqueria has been sold and my parents now work for Sam, too. We don't have to lie any more. They know what we do."

"What? When did this all happen?"

"Yesterday, they signed the papers and have their IDs. They will be trained soon. Until then we need to keep it quiet. Yasmene and Miguel will be recruited soon. Until they are on board, we need to keep it hush hush. Sandy and Junior need to keep it quiet too."

"Wow, they will be working with us. What will they do? Will they be flying with us?"

"No, they will be in charge of Food Services on Bear Island and live on the island."

"That is fantastic, what about the taqueria? Who bought it?" Dana asks.

We both laugh and I say, "Sam, of course! He made it happen so we can all be together, and we don't have to make up stories each time we have an assignment. It will make things a lot easier."

"Don't scare me like that again. Your parents are so nice to me," Dana says and turns his head away. I think we hurt his feelings.

When we arrive at Home Base Dana is over his hurt feelings and ready to find out what our next mission is. We are guided to Sam's office and Marilyn is already seated.

She smiles at us and says hello. Sam looks eager to get started so we sit next to Marilyn.

"Let's get started, here is a copy of the mission. Mary Ellen and Joy will be your leaders again. Joy will lead the rescue and Mary Ellen will lead the medical portion of the trip. You will leave here Friday morning, so make sure your schedules are clear. I know you hate missing classes but it's urgent you leave on Friday. Like I said, if you have any reading or work you need to do, you will have free time on the return flight."

Mary Ellen speaks up and says, "Make sure to bring any medications you may need, whatever your normal schedule is. I know last time there wasn't a problem. Just a reminder, there's always the possibility of the mission taking longer than expected. We should be back late Sunday night but plan ahead."

"Good idea, Mary Ellen. Bring enough meds and clothes to last you four days even though you'll only be gone for three full days. Joy will help you get an extra set of uniforms after the meeting. Keep everything in a go bag. It's easier if we have a mission at the last minute."

"Go ahead and read through the brief I gave you. It's easier to explain if you read and then ask questions."

We look at the copies we were given and start to read the itinerary.

Leave Oswego at seven am.

Flight should take about four hours.

Lunch and pick up 8 kids for transport.

Leave late afternoon for overnight flight to San Diego.

Deliver kids to our West Coast crew. They will escort them back to families.

Saturday morning: Fly to Brownsville and pick up fifty more kids from the same detention center as last time.

Saturday afternoon: Escort them to Bear Island Camp.

Saturday night: arrive at Bear Island Camp

Spend time with kids and relax.

Sunday afternoon: Return to Oswego.

"Any questions?" Sam asks as he looks directly at me.

"Yes, why are there more kids at the same detention center? Wasn't it closed down? The conditions were horrific."

"Another good question. But what is our mission?"

"To rescue those who can't rescue themselves."

"Exactly, it's not our mission to police the situation, it's our mission to rescue the kids in the detention centers. We already know this group of guards will leave if the cartel moves in. The less violence the better. So, we will keep trying to rescue those kids. We can't fight the cartel or change their behavior. The only thing we can do is rescue as many kids as possible before they are sold to traffickers," Sam explains.

"Sam, are government employees and border guards taking money for the kids?" Dana asks.

"Good question, Dana. They aren't. But the cartels come in and threaten them. In some cases they have killed some agents and border guards. They don't get the money, the cartels scare them away."

Marcos speaks up, "Why are we returning eight kids to San Diego when we picked them up in Texas? Will their parents be there or in Texas?"

"Some of those kids were trying to cross in Tijuana, Mexicali or Tecate. Four of the kids have parents who are American citizens and were picked up by mistake. We've located their families in San Diego. The four others are siblings, and their mother is in Tijuana waiting for them. She wants to return to Honduras. We will give them tickets and money to return home."

"Wouldn't it be easier on them to bring their mother here to Bear Island Camp?" I ask.

"No, at this moment we can only work on reuniting families at the border. It is unfortunate, but our goal is to help the kids. If they are better off with their parents in their hometown, we help get them there. If they are better off staying on Bear Island by themselves, we also look at that. Some parents are unable to feed their children, that's why they crossed the border in the first place. If it is a life or death situation, we opt to keep the child fed and housed. We do extensive interviews with the parents when we can contact them."

"You mean you won't return them to their parents if they don't want to go?" Dana asks.

"Do you decide if they get to go home or stay? I'm not comfortable with that. It's almost like playing God," Marcos says.

"Hold on, we are talking about extreme circumstances. You need to know the whole story before passing judgement. We have a team working on locating the parents, Many of the parents can't be located. We have prepared the facilities to have the kids grow up on Bear Island. If the parents are found, it's a different story. The decision-making team has been trained to make those choices, don't worry about the kids and families. We are trying our best to reunite them first."

Sam let that sink in before saying anything more. We were all quiet and thinking about some of the kids we had met. I hope Ricardo and Memo get to go back to their Papá and Abuelita. If they don't, I'm sure they will be sad. It will be nice to see them again this weekend.

"Finding those kids in the detention center was sad enough, now to think they will never find their parents is too much. Each mission will get harder," Marilyn says.

We are surprised to hear Marilyn speak up about this, she usually doesn't question Sam or his motives. She always defends his decisions and says Sam knows what he is doing. Is she questioning him?

Sam also looks surprised but says, "Marilyn, remember the kids who we are saving. Try to think of the joy on their faces when you rescue them and get them on that plane to Bear Island. It is such a relief that caring people show up to help them. Remember that, hold on to that thought."

"I'll   try.   It   is   sad   though."

CHAPTER 6

We arrive early Friday morning at the airstrip outside of town. Mary Ellen and Sam are in their car. The door to the plane remains closed. They don't get out of the vehicle until after we have been in the parking lot for fifteen minutes. I wonder what is happening and if maybe the mission might be cancelled.

Dana says, "Maybe they are changing the flight plan. Maybe something came up or changed since we last talked.

Just as he says that the door to the plane opens and we are told we can board. Eagerly we run up the steps to get into a warmer plane. We are all still suspicious and curious to what might be happening.

Sam and Mary Ellen get out of their car as another car pulls up. We see Joy is in the car that just approached. She is limping a little as she walks up to Sam and Mary Ellen.

Both Sam and Mary Ellen give Joy a big hug. Joy lifts her pant leg to show her ace-bandaged ankle. Sam gives her another hug. I wonder what is going on. Joy doesn't seem her normal self.

They all walk to the plane and come up the steps. Sam walks behind Joy in case she stumbles. Marcos, Dana and I rush to them to ask what happened.

"I'm alive. Give me some space," Joy smiles and moves to the first seat.

"There was an incident this morning, we'll give you all of the details in a minute. Gather around so you can all hear me. The nurses and helpers aren't within earshot and they don't need to hear the details."

"This morning Joy was out on an early run and someone tried to attack her," Sam explains. "As you can see, she is okay but got injured in the scuffle."

"Joy, what happened?" Dana asks.

"She has had a stalker and we thought we had taken care of him. She changed her running route and we have had a security detail car following her when she runs. This morning, because of our mission, she went out earlier than planned. Our security guy wasn't there yet, and she left on her own. You all have to listen to me when I tell you to be careful. If I send security out to watch you, pay attention. It's for a reason," Sam says as he raises his voice.

"Today Joy will accompany you on the mission, but she can't be lead. Mary Ellen will continue to be your healthcare lead. Margarita, you will take Joy's place today. You will handle the money and lead the group. Are you up for it? I'm asking you rather than Marilyn because of your ability to speak Spanish. Marilyn, it has nothing to do with your abilities," Sam says.

Marilyn answers, "It makes total sense Sam. Don't worry."

I see Marcos start to answer and then stop himself. I say, "Sam, if you think I'm ready for this I can do it. If you have any doubts please choose someone else." I say this with confidence to Sam but inside I'm a mess. What if

I can't do it? What if one of the kids gets hurt because of me? I may have a panic attack during the mission.

I look over at Marcos and he gives me a thumbs up and whispers, "It'll be ok,"

"Margarita, I wouldn't ask if I didn't think you were ready. Joy will brief you on the flight. You have quite a few hours of flight to make sure you understand what is expected. She will also tell you how to abort the mission if you need to. Joy has trained you well and your training will get put to good use today."

Marcos still looks uneasy; he is trying to encourage me but I know he is worried. We all carry our weapons on every mission, so I have back up if need be. Sam instructs us to go sit down and prepare for take-off. He hands Joy the mission packet and the money. Mary Ellen sits next to Joy and Sam exits the plane.

"Wheels up in a few minutes," Joy says in a loud voice. "Find your seats and get your seatbelts on. This is going to be a long ride. First stop, Halifax. Then to Bear Island for a pick-up. Sleep now if you need to."

The first thing Marcos says when we buckle up is, "Are you sure you are ready for this? If you aren't, just say so. Don't do it just because Sam asked you. Remember I'm here to help if you need it."

"I'm not doing that, if he thinks I'm ready, I'm ready. I know Joy will tell me what to do and tell me what to expect. Of course, I'm nervous, but a little excited at the same time. Relax, I can do it," I say with more confidence than I really have.

"I know you can do it. You crossed half a continent by yourself in a Greyhound bus. You are awesome! I just don't want anything to happen to you. We've got a lot of living to do yet," he says as he leans in to give me a hug. Dana and Marilyn look over at us, but since they know us so well, they probably know what we are talking about. They just smile and close their eyes to rest.

It's an easy flight and before I know it the captain is telling us we are twenty minutes out from Halifax. Joy calls me up to sit with her. Marcos stays behind because he knows I want to do this on my own.

"Okay, I'll walk you through the first part. When we land, customs officials will come aboard and ask for passports because we are entering Canada. Here is the envelope with all of our paperwork. Open it and take out the passport envelope, you don't need to do anything except hand it to them when they ask. If they ask if we are carrying any produce, weapons, drugs or anything that needs to be declared you hand them this packet. It declares all of our weapons and the medical supplies we carry onboard. We have permission to carry our weapons locked away while in flight. All of the medical supplies have already been declared. We have a special permission for that too."

"Do I need to say anything to them?" I ask.

"Let them do the talking. They have a job to do and they just want us to answer questions, they don't need conversation. You can be polite, act normal."

By the time we land and pull up to a designated spot on the runway, the captain tells the flight attendants to open the doors and let immigration and customs enter. Within five minutes, four Canadian agents are coming up the steps.

I unbuckle my belt and prepare to handle the first part of my mission. I now can say, my mission. The first time I'm lead person in a mission that helps children. It is scary, but very exciting at the same time. I see the agents walk toward Joy and me. I stand to greet them. When they ask for our paperwork and passports, I hand them the first envelope. One guard opens it while two other guards count the number of passengers. The two agents in front of me open the passport package and count passports and compare to the number the other two agents give them. They don't seem worried about matching our passports to each person, only if the number of passengers match the number of passports. We seem to meet their approval; they smile as they hand the package back to me.

The second agent takes over and asks if we are carrying any weapons, drugs, produce or plants. I hand them the envelope with the paperwork for our arms that are locked away during flight. This time they ask for me to open the lockbox. Joy hands me the key and tells me it is above us in the luggage rack. I stand and reach up to grab the lockbox. All of the agents are taller than I am, and one reaches up to help me bring the box down. I hand him the key and he opens the box. Inside all of the weapons and ammo match the manifest I gave him. He counts the weapons and snaps a picture. He also takes a picture of the manifest with the serial numbers.

"We need to do this in case any weapons show up in a crime or if you report them lost. We want to know right away if any weapons go missing while you are in Canada. Do you understand?" He asks me directly.

"Yes, I understand." He hands me a card with numbers to call if weapons are lost or stolen.

"Enjoy your time in Canada. You are in transit, is that correct?"

"Yes, we are in transit to Bear Island. We will be there for a short time and return tomorrow with some passengers. Our job is to transport passengers safely."

"Okay, good luck. Have a good day," he says as he hands back all of our paperwork.

"Thank you, you too," I say as I smile.

Time wasters they are not. Very efficient with their time. I guess they would have to be because of so many planes landing here.

Within the next twenty minutes we are all seated again, and on our way to Bear Island Camp. I haven't looked to see what the names are of the kids who we will transport to San Diego. I know it probably won't be Ricardo and Memo because their dad isn't an American Citizen. They are the two boys we bonded with from the last mission. Memo was so sick and Ricardo was so worried. Sam said the kids we would transport are mostly American citizens who got caught up with the others when their parents were picked up by ICE. It was all a big mistake for those families, not unlike the others. But these families found a way to get their kids back.

Sam also said a few of the kids were going back to Tijuana because their mother was located. It can't be Ricardo and Memo because he said mother, and from Honduras. They only have a dad and an abuelita. Somehow, I don't think Sam will find their family.

CHAPTER 7

We land on the airstrip on Bear Island before noon. I think we are all excited to see some of the kids again, see how they are doing and enjoy the time here. Dana and Marcos are in a hurry to see Ricardo and Memo. I am too, but they seem to have bonded a little more with Ricardo because he is older than most. We are all worried about Memo.

Joy explains to me what needs to be done while we are here. She gives me the instructions and says I am in charge of everything. I need to make sure we pick up the right kids, get the right paperwork and assign the kids to an adult in our crew. We want them to be comfortable on the flight.

I stand up and give instructions to everyone when we land. Mary Ellen yields to my instructions even though she is much more experienced.

"We will only be on the ground here for an hour or two. We need to get the following done while we are here and find the eight kids we are transporting, try to bond with them and make sure we have all of their paperwork. They will want to say goodbye to their friends here, some may be hesitant to leave. They found a comfortable place here."

"I'll assign you each a group. It's your job to find them and get them ready to depart in one hour. We have people on the ground who have almost everything prepared, but I'm sure the kids will drag their feet a little. Bear Island Camp is a nice place to stay. We have one sibling group. One of you will have four of from the same family returning to Tijuana so they can fly home to Honduras. Questions?"

"Margarita, will we have time to go see how Ricardo and Memo are doing?" Dana asks.

Marilyn also asks," I'd like to go see Adriana and Rosa. I want to check on them. I hope we have time."

"Yes, you'll have time but only about ten minutes. We have to focus on the ones we are transporting today. Tell them we will be back on Sunday. You might have a little more time then. Is everyone ready?" I ask.

"Yes," I hear everyone answer.

One of the nurses asks if there are any children in need of medical care on this flight to San Diego. I answer that they are fine and don't need medical care. "The ones we pick up tonight will most likely need some extra care. Just like the last flight."

Some of the nurses were with us on the last mission, but some stayed on Bear Island. The new ones ask the experienced ones what to expect. I watch as the rookies get filled in by the more experienced.

"We have exactly two hours here. Let's see if we can get out of here by 2:15. That means you all need to be back here ready to board at 2:00. Let's go get our kids," I say.

Everyone stands up and starts toward the exit door of the plane. I stay seated with Joy until everyone is off the plane. I wonder if I have said the right things. I look to Joy for reassurance.

"So far so good, Margarita. Your real test will be tonight when we pick up our next group. You'll do fine. They are aware we are showing up and know about what time. Our contact will be looking for his envelope of money and you'll hand it to him. Any questions?" Joy says.

"What if they ask for more money? What do I do?" I ask.

"We've talked about this. We have fifty-thousand dollars for fifty kids. If they give us more kids, we may have to pay more. We won't leave anyone behind. But, we aren't paying extra. The amount has been agreed upon already. Sam handled that. If they refuse, we'll discuss it. We aren't leaving there without those kids, but we also aren't going to cave to their expectations every time we make a trip. Got it?" Joy says.

"Yes, I've got it. Fifty kids for fifty thousand," I say.

I have to remind myself we aren't buying children. We are saving them from the traffickers. The cartels often buy the kids for trafficking from detention centers. They buy children, we don't. We rescue children from a life of slavery. I gather my things and stand to get off the plane. Joy does the same. She winces when she stands up; her ankle must really hurt.

"Joy, do you want me to help you? Here lean on my arm," I say.

"No, I can do it. You go ahead and I'll catch up with you," she answers.

I feel bad leaving her behind, but I am eager to get off the plane and see the kids. When I step down on Bear Island I relax. It is such a calming atmosphere. The combination of the tall fir trees, the water lapping at the shore and the fresh air makes me want to live here forever. It looks like I'll get that chance now that Sam has hired my parents.

As I walk toward the main lodge called the Log Cabin, I see Marcos and Dana in the distance. Ricardo, Adriana and Rosa are walking with them. They all look happy to see Marcos and Dana again. I wonder where Memo is; is it possible he is still in the infirmary? I hope not. So many of these kids will have trauma from their separation from their families. I wonder what Sam and Mary Ellen have planned to help them.

Adriana and Rosa run to me when they see me. "Margarita, we've been looking for you, we missed you. When we saw Marcos and Dana, we were surprised you weren't here."

Rosa says, "I feel so much better, but Memo is still in the infirmary. I think he is really sick."

I look at Ricardo to see his reaction to Rosa's comment. His head droops, his eyes are misty, and he doesn't look like he wants to talk about it.

"Ricardo, how are you? How is Memo?" I ask.

He probably already told Dana and Marcos. I look around and wonder where Marilyn and Mary Ellen are. They must be working with the paperwork for the children we are transporting.

"Margarita, Memo is still not talking. The doctors say he needs to rest, and he might start talking. We still don't know what happened while he was in the detention center. He and Rosa are the only ones who can tell us what really happened," Ricardo says.

I hug him and say, "I'm so sorry Ricardo. It has to be so hard for you. Has anyone located your papá or abuelita?"

"No, they don't know anything yet. They are still looking. Some people have talked with their families."

"Yes, we are transporting eight kids today. That's why we are here. Our goal is to help you and the other kids find your families," I explain.

Marcos looks at me and signals we need to get going. I nod and tell the kids we need to look for the ones we are transporting.

Ricardo follows us to the infirmary. Rosa and Adriana walk toward the Log Cabin. They both are helping in the kitchen today. To think that soon my family will be here and work with all of these kids makes me smile. I hope Sandy and Junior will adapt.

I find Marilyn and Mary Ellen in the office. They have five kids with them, and the doctor is giving instructions for each child. He is concerned the parents may not follow up with the suggested medications and explains to Marilyn how to give explicit instructions. I watch as the younger kids play with toys on the floor. The siblings are listening to instructions while the doctor tells Marilyn. A translator helps translate for the kids.

The doctor hands Marilyn a drawstring bag with a tag for each child. The tag has each child's name and age. Inside the bag there are prescriptions to last three months for each child. Also, instructions on what will happen if certain prescriptions are discontinued.

Marilyn introduces me to the children and tells me which ones are siblings. I greet them and tell them we are all leaving soon. We need to get back in the air if we are to keep on schedule.

"Marilyn, will you be finished with the doctor in five minutes? We need to get to lunch. We have a schedule to keep," I whisper.

"Yes, we should be finished here, and the kids have said their goodbyes to their friends here on the island. It's sad, but they are excited to be reunited with their families. I'm glad they haven't stayed longer. I think it's going to be harder for the kids who really start making friends and settle in here at Bear Island Camp," Marilyn says.

Ten minutes later we are all seated and eating lunch. The kids who we will transport are seated with us. We want to save time by keeping the kids with us.

After lunch we gather near the golf carts in front of the Log Cabin Lodge. We load the kids and all of us into four golf carts and start down the hill toward the small bus to the airstrip. Lunch is just starting for everyone else. They all come and follow us down to the parking lot. They are excited and tearful at the same time. They are sending some of their friends back home to their families. Some hope they will be next, others hope they will never leave Bear Island. It's a mixture of joy and sorrow. This will leave forty-two kids on Bear Island. Little do they know that tomorrow we'll be back with fifty more. The staff is aware and preparing for their arrival, but the children have no idea they will share their paradise with fifty new kids. Who knows how many will come in the next few weeks?

CHAPTER 8

We taxi the runway and soon we are in the air. Marilyn and Dana sit with the older kids and help them get settled. The nurses on board and Mary Ellen take the younger ones to the back where they normally have the sick kids. There is more room and they can put the little ones down for a nap where they are more comfortable.

Joy and I once again review what happened so far on our mission and what we still need to accomplish.

"Good job, you got us off the ground on time and we are on schedule. That is a tough part of each mission, trying to get everyone where they need to be and on time. Sometimes it's like herding cats, but you did a great job. It doesn't hurt that you are all friends and know each other so well. This is a tight group and easier to manage. Keep in mind if you are asked to work with a different team it may not be as easy," Joy says.

"Why would I work with another team?" I ask.

"If Sam sees you can handle a team and he needs a leader, he may ask you to lead a different group. It probably won't happen so early on, but later you may be promoted to permanent lead. Then you may be asked to help other teams. You are an important part of Sam's team. He trusts you," Joy adds.

"I'm flattered, but I hope I only have to work with this team. I feel more comfortable with my team."

"Well, you never know what Sam might ask you to do. I'm sure he'll try to keep you all together. But maybe he will train you all as leaders," Joy says.

"I hadn't thought of that. Everything is moving so fast. This is only our second mission and I'm already acting lead. What an experience!" I exclaim.

I sit back and don't know what to think. How did this all happen? I went from being an orphan in Baja to now leading a top-secret team on a rescue mission. It all happened in such a short time. Baja, Woodburn, Fish Camp, Orcas Island, SUNY at Oswego and now I'm leading a team to help rescue kids from a detention camp on the border. Nothing I could have ever imagined.

I also think of when I first met Marcos, who was called Teodoro at the time. How kind he was to me. He helped me and then we fell in love and got married. I can't imagine my life without him. I turn to look at him seated a few rows back. He is looking out the window but quickly looks up front and we lock eyes. We both smile. Maybe he's thinking of the same thing?

The flight to Halifax is only a couple of hours but I decide to take a short nap. I need to be alert and at the top of my game when immigration comes on board. I have a feeling returning these kids to the States isn't going to be as easy as it was taking them out of the country. I close my eyes and try to nap.

I open my eyes when the captain comes on the radio and says, "Twenty minutes to approach to Halifax. Prepare for landing."

I look over at Joy and she smiles at me, "This is you, kid. Do you know what to do?"

"Yes, I've got the envelope here. Four passports for the kids returning to their families. Transport visas for the four who will return to Mexico. Is there anything I should know to say or not say?" I ask.

"No, it's pretty cut and dried. The only question they should have is how many kids we are transporting. Do you have the team's paperwork too? They'll ask about that."

"Yes, here in a separate packet. Passports for everyone on board. I'm kind of like a travel agent here," I joke.

"Yeah, if a travel agent carried a gun and helped rescue kids from a detention center," Joy says with a laugh.

"True. But this part seems relatively easy," I say.

"Not easy, Sam just has a crackerjack team that puts all of the paperwork together. Some of the paperwork here can take months. His team can expedite visas and passports when needed. Without Sam's help, these kids wouldn't be returning to their families ever. It's possible they would have been sold to the highest bidder. Remember there are some evil people working in the border area. The government agents who are assigned to the detention centers don't want to battle with the cartels. They are paid off to leave and the people from the cartel move in to sell them and make more money. They might have been sold into slavery. Don't ever forget about that. We can joke about our jobs, but what we are doing is saving kids from trafficking," Joy reminds me.

"Believe me, I know Sam has helped a lot of people. I never forget where I came from and where I could have ended up. My Tío Enrique would have sold me off in a minute. I was lucky to get away. I'll never forget the people who helped at Fish Camp. That is where I found a way to get my freedom from Tío Enrique."

The plane lands and some of the kids think we are already in California. I can see the excitement on their faces. I also see the disappointment when Dana tells them we are still in Canada and have to fly all night to get to California.

Immigration and customs are aboard as soon as the doors open. They don't want us taking up runway space either. If we are carrying too many kids or if there are kids without passports or visas, they know it will be a long process. I see the look of relief on their faces when I hand them the packet of passports and visas.

"How many children are you transporting?" The agent asks after looking through the employee passports.

"We have four American citizens and four with transport visas. Those four are returning to Mexico. They won't be staying in the US," I say with confidence.

"What assurances do you have that they won't stay? How do we know they won't get off the plane in California and stay?" He asks.

I hesitate for a moment and say, "The transit visas are the documents that my boss requested for them to re-enter the country via the US. We have two agents on the ground in San Diego who will transport those four back across the border to Tijuana. Their mother is waiting there," I respond.

Before he can ask, I pull out the instructions for transport from San Diego Airport, the names of the two agents who will escort them to Tijuana and phone numbers to call.

"Here are the two agents who will pick them up at the airport and transport them. Here are two contact numbers if you need to call. Also, here is my boss' emergency contact if there is any question," I say calmly.

"That's not necessary. If you transport more kids back to Mexico, you can save time by adding that paperwork with the visas. Everything is in order. Have a great flight," he says as he hands all the paperwork back to me.

The other agents in the meantime have counted the number aboard and spoken to each one. It appears everything is okay, and we can soon take off.

"One more thing, how is it that someone so young is leading this group? You look like you should be in high school not in charge of an operation like this," he asks.

"I'm just lucky, I guess. I've been very lucky," I smile.

"Have a safe trip, will we see you here again?" He asks.

"We never know, maybe," I laugh.

After the attendant closes the doors and we taxi down the runway Joy leans over and says, "Excellent job, it looks like you've been doing this for years. You'll be permanent lead in no time."

But do I want that? I want to spend time with Marcos and my family, I'm not sure I want to lead these operations all the time. I always imagined working for the FBI in the forensics department and going home every night. I never imagined flying across country with a gun at my hip. Is this what I really want?

Bear Island Camp

CHAPTER 9

The attendants bring us an early dinner. After they pick up our trays they dim the lights so we can sleep. The cartoons are on non-stop for the flight but most of us are asleep and unaware of the movie screen. The nurses in the back of the plane attend to the little ones.

We are served a snack when we are about two hours out from San Diego. It's funny how hungry I get just sitting on an airplane doing nothing. I wonder if the others are just as hungry. I change my seat to move back to sit with Marcos, Dana and Marilyn. The kids who were sitting with them have moved to have more room to themselves.

Marcos smiles as I sit next to him. "How are you, boss?" He kids as he gives me a kiss on the cheek.

"Stop, I'm not your boss. I just handle the paperwork and make sure everyone has a passport. Besides if I were your boss you wouldn't be able to kiss me."

"You are our boss when we get to the detention center, there you are the one to deal with the guards there. Then you are the boss. We follow your directions the minute we enter the facility. If you tell us to abort the mission, we do. You call the shots. But I doubt you will have any problems. I know Joy has probably briefed you, so you know what to expect."

"Yes, she has. I never knew how much she did. She has a lot of responsibility. The weapons, the passports, the kids, the team and on top of that handing over the money to the guards. She is training me. She says we might all become permanent leaders and work with different teams," I say.

"What? I don't want to work with another team," Dana says.

"I don't either, I like our team," Marcos says.

Marilyn, who is always the sensible one, says, "If Sam asks you to lead another team it's because he needs you. You all know you'll do whatever he asks."

"True, but I don't like the idea. I like working with people I know," Dana says.

When we finish our snack we decide to check on the kids. Dana and Marcos move over to sit with the three older ones. Marilyn and I go to check on the younger kids. When we come back, we hear the conversation between Dana and the kids.

"Are you excited to meet up with your parents again?" Dana asks them.

"Well, yes but at the same time I was having fun at Bear Island. I wish I could stay there, and they could come and live there too. I don't really want to live in San Diego," the oldest says.

"Really? Why not?" He asks.

"It's hot, and there's too many people. We live in an apartment. I liked living in the woods on Bear Island. It was so much fun. There was no traffic and people are nice there. In San Diego sometimes I get picked on at school, but that didn't happen there. My English is better now, but some kids make fun of me because they say I don't say words right. I don't like that," he says.

"Well, remember you are bilingual. You speak two languages. Every day your English will get a little better and before you know it no one will notice, and they'll stop making fun of you. I wish I spoke Spanish," Dana says.

"You do? Why?" He asks.

"Because I could communicate with so many more people. Now, if I travel or meet someone who speaks Spanish and doesn't speak English, I have no chance of getting to know them. Like you, I wouldn't be able to talk to you," Dana explains.

"I never thought of it that way. You mean if I speak two languages, I'll meet more people? Or talk with more people?" He asks.

"Yes, absolutely. You'll be able to read and write more too. Not all books written in Spanish are translated into English. There are a lot of books you could read that other people won't be able to."

"Thanks. So, you think things will get better? I'll be able to learn English and join the basketball team and stuff like that?" he asks.

'Why not? Of course, you can. Do you like basketball?" Dana asks.

"Yeah, but in our neighborhood only the older kids play. They don't let us play; they say we are too short. But on Bear Island there was a basketball court for everyone. Everyone got to play. Sometimes we took turns, the older kids and then the younger kids. But at least they let us play. I liked it there, but I did miss my parents."

"Well, now you've been away for a while you might have a different outlook. Maybe you'll get the younger kids together and start your own games. Is there another court near your apartments?"

"Yeah at the middle school, maybe we can go there. I hadn't thought that. I just thought about playing at our apartment complex."

"Maybe one of the dads can help you guys get organized. Go for a few times to make sure you have enough people to play. Lay down some rules too. It always helps to have a coach," Dana smiles and pats the boy on his back.

I realize there is so much more to this job than just transporting these kids. They have been through so much and now it may be even more difficult for them. They have the separation trauma from when their parents were detained, and they were separated. Now they might feel guilty because they felt safe on Bear Island Camp. They have a lot of issues to work through. I hope, when they are reunited with their families, they can get some counseling to help them through it. I wonder if people who don't know about Bear Island Camp will believe them when they talk about their experiences. Maybe they will think they made it up to cope with the separation. I hope they find some caring counselors.

The captain comes back on and tells us to prepare for landing. I move back to the front with Joy. Maybe she has some last-minute details to share with me. I buckle in and Joy smiles at me.

"Are you ready for this? There is going to be a lot of emotion. Pinch yourself if the tears start. It might help. It helps for me sometimes. When we arrive, we will pull on to a smaller runway. The agents picking up the kids with families in San Diego will be in one van. The other van will be there to take the four who are going back across to Tijuana. Let's make sure before the kids get off the plane that the kids returning to Mexico know their mother won't be here. Let's have them deplane first and that van will move away. It will save a lot of tears," Joy says.

"I hadn't thought of that. That's a good idea! When we land, I'll make sure the kids get to say good-bye to each other and then take the first four off the plane before the others. We'll hand them over to agents in the van and make sure they understand what is happening," I say.

"Yes, that works," Joy responds.

"I need to fill in the others on what will happen before we exit the plane. They need to know."

"You'll have time. When the plane lands and we taxi to the runway, you can move back to talk with them. You, Dana, Marcos and Marilyn will walk two kids off the plane. Hold their hands and walk them to the van. Have Marcos and Dana take the first group to the van returning to Mexico. If the other van is there, make sure they don't get the wrong van," Joy says.

"How will we know?" I ask.

"You run ahead and make sure which one is taking the four kids to Mexico. Then you signal them to bring them to the van. If anyone gets out of the other van, you make sure they get back in. Threaten them if you have to, they are not to get out of the van until they see their own kids. Ask the agents to make sure they stay put until you bring their kids to them. If one mother decides to jump out of the van, the four going to Mexico are going to wonder why their mother didn't come to get them. Understand?"

"Yes, understood," I say.

This may be very sad. I need to prepare myself to say good-bye to these kids.

Bear Island Camp

CHAPTER 10

The plane lands and we taxi down to a distant runway away from the terminal. I look out the window and see two vans parked on the runway. I guess I will have to run over to check on which van is the correct one.

I walk back to the seat where Marcos, Dana and Marilyn are seated and explain to them what needs to happen. Marcos and Dana will escort the four children to the van and hand them over to agents. It is sure to be a tear-jerker. I don't think pinching myself will stop the tears. I tell them to go to the back of the plane and let the kids know what is going to happen and to start their goodbyes with each other. I'm sure there will be tears there too.

I prepare to deplane as soon as the door is opened. The portable stairway is already in place.

As I walk down the stairs it is obvious which van carries the parents. I see anxious families with balloons and stuffed animals. They are waving and asking the guards in their van if they can get out and come over to the plane. I see their faces drop after getting the answer.

The two agents exit the other van and hand me paperwork proving they are connected to Sam Mason and the destination for these four children is Tijuana. They have instructions to only hand them over to their mother no one else.

"Have you had contact with their mother? Do you know where she is staying? Do you have an address?" I ask.

"Yes, of course. She is meeting us at the airport. Sam gave them all tickets to fly back to Honduras. They want to return home and never cross the border again. They have suffered so much, they just want to return to their small casita and work. We will accompany them until they are on the plane. Once they are on the plane and in the air our mission is over."

"It looks like Sam organized this very well," I say.

"He always does, there is no doubt about it," the agent answers.

I turn around to see Marcos and Dana walking toward us. Marcos has the three-year old by the hand and Dana is holding the one-year old. The two older ones hold each others' hands. I know there will be tears when they hand them over.

Dana hands the one-year old to the agent and they both help buckle her into the car-seat. He backs away and then turns to me with tears in his eyes. Marcos picks the little one holding his hand up and places him in the next car seat. He doesn't wait to help buckle the child in, he turns and walks toward Marilyn after hugging good-bye to the other kids. I don't think he wants me to see his tears. I check to make sure the agents have everything they need, and they give me a thumbs up. I close the sliding door on the van and back away. I say a little prayer and hope these children arrive safely back in their moms' arms today. We wave as the van drives away.

Marcos and Dana walk back to the plane. I try to pinch myself; I can't start crying yet. Our mission isn't complete. The others try to remain professional and ask me what to do next.

"Okay, now it's Marilyn's and my turn. These parents have waited long enough. Marcos, tell the agents they can let them get out of the van while we get the kids. This is going to be hard on all of us, so pinch yourselves if you think you are going to cry," I say.

"What good will that do?" Marco asks.

"I don't know, Joy told me that and it worked for me so far. I don't think it's going to work for much longer though," I say as I look away. I don't want to look into Marco's eyes. I know I'll lose it if I do.

Marilyn and I see the four kids at the top of the steps. They have already seen their parents. Marilyn grabs the two smallest kids and walks them down the stairs. Marilyn walks at a normal pace toward the parents. I think she's had too many good-byes in her life and has adopted a stoic response to the situation.

I walk hand in hand with the other two until they drop my hand and start running to their parents. They are so excited they can't wait to be back with their parents.

I greet the parents and say, "Please remember, your children have been through a lot. They may not respond like you remember them. Just love them and hug them. If they don't seem happy to see you it's because they have been through so much. They have been safe snd now they are here safe with you. It will take some time to adjust," I say.

They listen but I'm not sure they hear what I say. The next thing I hear screams and loud kisses.

"¡Mamá!, !Papá!"

All of the balloons and stuffed animals don't mean a thing at this moment. They all want to hug and kiss each other. The separation has been too long.

One father is swinging their child around in circles, the other won't let go of his child. The mothers are crying and saying, "Gracias a Dios. ¡Qué alegria!

I look back at the plane and I see Joy standing in the doorway.

We all step back and try to look professional. I watch to see what the agents in the van will do. They get out and hand me similar paperwork as the other agents. These families are American citizens that got caught up in the immigration sweep. These four kids never crossed the border, they were born in the US. None of the kids should have ever ended up in detention centers, but these four had no reason at all.

The children appear very happy to see their parents. After a few minutes I see one boy turn and look at Marcos. His smile disappears and he runs over to give Marcos a hug. He jumps into Marcos's arms. Marcos is so surprised he picks him up and gives him a huge bear hug. The other kids run to Dana, Marilyn and me. They thank us all for helping them get back to their parents. I think we can pinch ourselves all we want, there is no way of stopping those tears now.

We watch from the steps of the plane as the van disappears. Some of the children are still waving as the van gets smaller and smaller in the distance. This was difficult for all of us, but the kids are better off with their families than on Bear Island.

We need to get back in the air and head for Texas. Those kids in the detention center don't know we are coming, but we want to get there as soon as we can. Our flight from San Diego to Brownsville will take about four hours. The adrenaline rush will keep us awake, but we all know we need to sleep. Each couple finds seats and settles in for a nap. We will need to be alert on our flight from Brownsville to Bear Island Camp. This is our second time flying that trip. The first time it was all a dream because we were so excited for the kids. We watched them as they got to put on clean clothes, eat a hot meal and even have ice cream. I hope this trip goes as well as the first one.

I rest my head on Marco's shoulder and we share a blanket. Both of our seats recline, and we are quite comfortable. I hope I can sleep.

Before I know it, I hear a beep from the captain's microphone. He comes on and says, "Folks, we are about one hour out from Brownsville. Just want to give you the heads up. Continue napping or grab something to eat. We'll be on the ground in about an hour."

I look over at Marcos and he is trying to fall back to sleep. I snuggle in closer and do the same, but I hear the others are asking for their lunch. What do I prefer? More sleep or to eat a hot meal? I know the answer, but also know we need to be at the top of our game. I decide to ask the attendant for our dinners too. Marcos says he wants to sleep more, and he dozes until the food arrives. As soon as the food is placed in front of him, he pulls his seat up and sits up to eat.

We both look at the food and realize it is roasted chicken, mashed potatoes and gravy and corn. It looks delicious. I wasn't hungry until now, but it smells so good. We both dig in and are quiet. We look at each other and smile, it is delicious. I hear Marilyn say from the back, "This isn't airline food. I've never had such delicious food on an airplane."

I have to agree with her. On our flight from Orcas Island to New York the food wasn't identifiable let alone delicious. Sam definitely makes sure everyone is taken care of. As we finish, the attendant brings us chocolate ice cream for dessert. This raises our spirits. I finish and tell Marcos I need to go sit with Joy to make sure I know everything I need to.

I lean over and give him a kiss on the cheek. He pulls me into a hug and says, "I'm so proud of you and happy I met you." I don't want to leave his hug but I stand up and walk to the front of the plane.

Joy is finishing her dinner and looks like she took a nap as well. I wonder if she needed any help. I should have asked. But I wanted to spend time with Marcos and also get a nap.

"Did you get a chance to rest?" Joy asks.

"Yes, we both took a short nap and we ate dinner. We want to be at our best when we pick up the kids. Anything new I need to know about?" I ask.

"Well, it looks like we have more sick kids on this trip. Could you go back and ask Mary Ellen and the nurses to come up front please?"

"Sure," I say as I look at her nervously. What kind of sick, I wonder?

The nurses and helpers come to the front and sit near Joy. I stand in front to give them more room. I didn't realize we had this many medical staff on board. I knew the number of passengers, but I didn't realize they were all medically trained. We have two doctors on board as well. I think the last trip we only had one doctor and a few nurses.

Joy tries to stand but we tell her to stay seated. Some stand in the seats behind Joy so they can hear.

"This trip is a little different from the last. We just got word that some of the kids are quite sick with vomiting and diarrhea. Let's see if we can get prepared before we land. I've ordered two buses the same as last time. This time let's put all of the sick kids in one bus, keep the healthy ones away from them. The kids are going to fight it, we know. They will want to be reunited with their siblings. But it's important we try to keep them separated.

We don't know what type of illness these kids have. Doctors, we will look to you for advice once we get the kids aboard the plane. I say one of you go with us to pick up the kids, the other stays here with a nurse and prepares IVs and antibiotics. We will want to treat them as soon as we get them on board. Let's also keep the rear restrooms open for those kids. If what they say is true, we may have over half of the kids sick. Let's try to keep the others up front. They all will get a check-up before we land in Halifax, but we want to treat the sickest kids first. It it's the flu or a stomach bug we can treat them. But if it's something more serious like hepatitis or worse we need to be careful to contain it as much as possible. The kids have been in horrible conditions so they all may soon be sick. Let's do our best, okay?"

The two doctors agree and decide between them which one will stay aboard and prep. One doctor speaks up and says, "Okay, we all need to wear gloves. Face masks if we determine it is something highly contagious. The most probable is that the kids are more susceptible because of their compromised immune systems. But gloves for all and masks if you choose. I know the masks may be scary for the kids. Take one with you, if I give a signal to mask up make sure you do. It probably is a stomach bug, but let's be cautious."

I look at Joy and think I thought this mission would be the same as the last. It appears it will be nothing like the last one. I go back to inform the team. They look worried when I tell them. I get them a box of gloves and face masks for each one.

"Put the mask in your pocket unless you want to wear it from the beginning. Gloves on at all times. These kids are sicker than the last group. Over half of them will be separated and put in the back of the plane. We are to keep the healthier ones up front and away from the others. They also will be in two separate buses. Let's help the kids understand why. Tell them they'll be reunited when we get to Bear Island. Any questions?"

Marcos asks, "Margarita, are you okay? You look a little scared."

"I'm fine. I just didn't think these kids would be sick. They may be vomiting and have diarrhea. The flight to Halifax may not be as restful as the last one. It's too bad we don't have showers on the plane or have time for them to shower. I'm sure they would feel better. Next trip maybe we should ask Sam if we can work something out," I answer.

"Let's get back to our seats. We'll be on final approach to Brownsville soon," I say.

I stay up front with Joy and the others move up closer to sit behind us. We are all anxious to get those kids out of the detention center as fast as we can. Once we land, we still have thirty minutes by bus to get to the center. It will take us at least a half hour to get them out and loaded on the buses. It's too long for those kids, they need help now.

We land in Brownsville and taxi up to a gate only to be told we need to go back to the runway. Airport officials are aware of who we are and who we transport. They don't want us where anyone can see us. It's for the best. When we leave, we will drive the buses right out on to the runway. The captain takes us back out to a secluded runway. The two buses are waiting for us. Someone got the communication we would be deplaning on the runway even if we didn't.

Everyone grabs their things. I reach up to get the locked gun case in the overhead bin. I unlock it and each team member grabs their weapon and ammo. We all know who gets what now and we move quickly to get to the bus. One doctor, Mary Ellen and nurses follow us. They all carry supplies to help the kids while on the bus. The other doctor stays behind to prep the IVs and beds for the kids.

Once on the bus, we signal the driver to get us to the detention center as soon as possible. It's starting to get dark and it will be much easier if there is still daylight to work by. The silence on the bus is palpable. We are all quiet, each one with our own thoughts. The ride seems to take forever but we see the spinning car in a distance. I had forgotten about this used car lot with the spinning car in the air. I wonder what the kids thought of that when they saw it.

We finally approach the gate; this time it's open and there are no guards. Maybe they decided once they get the payment no need for the guards. When we roll up to the center, we can only see a four by four sitting near the door with one man. I step down from the bus with my teammates watching my back. The man steps out of the 4x4 and walks toward me.

"Everyone is gone here except for me and the kids. You took a lot longer than we expected. Our guys all got scared because the kids are sick. We're happy to turn them over to you. Where's the money?" He asks.

I hand him the briefcase with the fifty-thousand dollars and say, "How sick are they? Did you have a doctor come in to treat them?"

"No, we just hold them until either you or the others come to pick them up. I doubt the traffickers would want these kids, they are all yours," he says as he walks back to his vehicle.

"Wait, are you going to sanitize this place before you bring more kids? It probably needs it if they've been sick," I say.

"Yeah, we'll hose it down before the next group. It got stinky in there," he says.

"It needs to be disinfected. If these kids are sick the next group will be too," I say.

"You worry about what you do, and I'll worry about what I do, okay?" he says with a snarl. "Your job is to give me the money and take the kids. You are half done now, I have the money and the kids are yours," he says. I watch as he starts his vehicle and drives away.

The others are behind me now with their gear and we walk into the center. The smell of vomit and feces is very strong. The doctor tells us we will need gowns if we are going to carry the children. One of the nurses runs back to the bus and grabs a box of paper gowns. Another one is setting up a table with the clean shorts and t-shirts. I see she also has some sanitizing wipes and large rolls of paper towels. It's too bad we don't have a portable shower or even a hose.

We find the light switches and turn on all of the overhead lights. This wakes up the children who are sleeping. Some aren't sleeping and we hear crying from some of the cages. We open all of the doors and tell them to go outside and wait for us. The ones who can't walk we carry. Dana and Marcos start carrying the older ones who are weak and can't walk. Marilyn and I carry the younger ones. The little ones need diaper changes and it looks like they may not have been changed recently. Who does this to kids?

We bring them outside and the doctor and nurses are ready to do a quick once over. Their look of dismay is obvious. The doctor tells one of the aides to find a hose or bucket of water.

"These kids can't travel like this. Is there a shower facility inside?" He asks.

One of the kids points to the trailer parked near the far exit of the building, "We shower in there. But they keep it locked."

The doctor looks at Marcos and Dana and says, "Break the door down, get these kids a shower. No child should be this dirty. These people who kept them here are animals."

Marcos and Dana run over to try the doors on the shower unit. They are locked so Dana pulls out his weapon and fires a shot. The lock is destroyed, and the door flies open. Once inside they turn on the showers, look for soap and towels and get everything prepared.

When they return the doctor hands them all of the younger children. "These kids need it the most. Let's get them cleaned up and clothed. Then we can do a medical check. I'll keep half of the nurses here. All of the others go help these guys please. Let's get them human again."

The nurses split up, half run to the showers to help Marcos and Dana with the kids. Marilyn and I wait on the outside for the kids to come out in their towels. We dry them off and clothe them in their Bear Island shorts and t-shirts. Nurses come to us to carry the kids over to the doctor. The process of cleaning twelve younger children takes us almost thirty minutes. The kids look so relieved when they are dressed and clean.

After the twelve youngest ones are finished in the showers Marcos and Dana help the boys get cleaned up. Marilyn and I stand outside with the girls and let them know they are next. I tell them we'll clean the showers before they go in and not to worry. They are all embarrassed of the condition they are in. The older boys only take about fifteen minutes to exit and get their clothes on.

Marilyn and I go in to help Dana and Marcos clean the shower floors and spray disinfectant everywhere. The dirty paper suits and diapers are in a huge trash can. Dana takes it outside and disposes of it in a dumpster nearby.

The girls finally get their chance to clean up. Marilyn and I go in the showers with them and help them shampoo their hair and give them extra time to just stand under the showers. This is a relief for them, the first time in weeks they feel safe. They don't even know who we are, but they feel safe.

When the girls are given their clothes and hairbrushes, they walk toward the bus. Some arm in arm, others holding Marilyn's hand. They have been through a lot and a lot we probably will never know about.

Marcos and Dana don't bother to clean up the shower rooms after the girls leave. They say, "The guards can do that. They created this mess they can clean it up." Although I wonder if the next kids coming in will have to face this same mess. We can't worry about that now; we have fifty sick kids to move across the country to a new home.

CHAPTER 11

As the kids board the bus, each one is given two water bottles and a plain roll to eat. The doctor wants to make sure they can keep food down before giving them anything more. The babies and toddlers are given bottles of enriched water. The nurses and doctors are on one bus with the sick children and the team and I are on the second bus with the kids who are still healthy. We try to keep them from getting whatever the other kids have.

It's interesting to us that the majority of the kids who are sick are under the age of five. The older kids aren't as sick, and the teenagers seem to be healthy. They all tell us how worried they are about their younger siblings.

We explain to them we are going to help them the best we can. "Some of your siblings are very sick, but we have doctors and nurses who are here to help. We ask you stay away from your family members until we get to our destination. Then the doctors will let us know if you can see them."

"Where are we going? Are we going to meet up with our parents? We were separated and I'm not sure where my parents are," one young girl says. The other kids start to ask the same questions. I tell them when we are aboard the plane, we will let them know our plan.

"Plane, what plane? Where are you taking us? What if I don't want to get on another plane?" A teenage boy asks.

"We need to take you away from this horrible place and get to a safe place for you all. We have a safe place. Trust us, please. We aren't like the people who helped you across the border and then helped get you put into a detention center," I explain.

The kids sit back and quiet down. I don't think they are content with my answer, but they are probably too exhausted to fight. They really have been through too much for their young age. As we drive by the car spinning on top of a pole one of the kids says, "I remember that; I thought we were going to an amusement park when we passed it the first time. I was so wrong, that was no amusement park."

I feel bad for the disappointment these kids must feel every time someone lied to them or deceived them. I know exactly how they feel. My Tío Enrique was an expert in deception. I try not to think back to the times I was in a vulnerable situation like these kids. But helping them makes me feel like there is hope and there are always people who help if they can.

The bus bounces on the dirt road until we reach the highway. Once on the highway I can feel a sense of calm come over the kids and our team. That detention center is like a cloud of despair, only sad, sad things happen there. We drive another twenty minutes and drive right out to the plane waiting on the airstrip runway.

Joy is waiting in the doorway of the plane as we pull up. She signals for me to exit the bus first and meet with her. I question why because as I leave the bus the doctor also runs to catch up with me.

When I reach the top of the stairs Joy says, "They are sending a MediVac helicopter. We need to wait here. We can board the other kids but Margarita you need to choose one of your teammates to stay behind with the child."

"What? Why? What happened?"

"The doctor tried to text you from the other bus, but you had no coverage for a few minutes, so he texted me. We have two extremely ill kids on that bus. They have very high fevers. We need to get them to a hospital right away. We can't leave them here alone, so someone needs to stay with them with their paperwork. If they are left here alone, they will probably end up in another detention center when they are released."

"How should I do this? Ask for a volunteer? What would you do Joy?" I ask.

"It's up to you, you can ask for a volunteer or you can just pick one. You decide."

I turn to walk back to the bus and wonder what I should do. If I pick Marcos, he and I will be separated. If I pick either Marilyn or Dana, they will be separated. I can't stay because I'm in charge of the mission.

Marcos gets off the bus with Marilyn and Dana right behind him.

"Uh oh. I recognize that face. What's happening Margarita?" Marcos asks.

"Two kids are really sick and need to be taken by helicopter to the hospital. One of us needs to stay behind."

They all look at each other and I know they are thinking the same thing. Who wants to be separated from their partner and group?

Before I can say anything more Dana speaks up, "Do you mean if I stay, I get to fly in the helicopter with them?"

"Yes, you'll need to stay with them the whole time. Transportation will be sent to pick you up when the kids are better. Do you want to do that?" I ask as I glance at Marilyn.

"Well, I hate to leave Marilyn and you guys, but I would love to fly in a helicopter. It will be so cool," Dana answers.

"Dana, think about it. What if the kids are really sick and one of them dies? You will be here on your own. Do you want to do that?" Marilyn asks.

"I'd rather do it than have you do it. I'm sure Marcos would do the same for Margarita. The positive part of this whole sad mess is I get to fly in a MediVac helicopter. I don't want to abandon the mission, but I get to do something different," he answers.

"You might miss some classes," I say.

"It's okay. It's part of the mission and someone has to do it. I volunteer!"

"Thank you, Dana. I didn't know this would be part of being the leader. I didn't want to choose anyone to stay behind."

"Done, I'm it! Let's get these kids on the plane. Or do we have to wait for the helicopter?"

"No, we need to board all of the kids except for the two sickest ones. Apparently, they have a high fever and need to be hospitalized right away. The doctors said they are too sick to travel."

"Do they have siblings on the bus? What do we tell them?" Marcos asks.

"Yes, two siblings. They can choose to stay behind with you or board the plane. We are hoping they board the plane. It will be easier to keep them healthy, fed and taken care of. We need to identify who the siblings are and talk to them. Let's get the kids aboard the plane and I'll ask Joy who the two are. Then you and I can talk to the siblings, okay Dana?" I ask.

"Sure thing. Let's see what they have to say," he says.

Joy texts me the two names and I look to see if I recognize who it might be. On the last trip we got to know the kids more. This time because of the showers and chaos when we arrived at the detention center I didn't get to know as many kids.

"Dana, we need to find Cielo and Raul. They are the two siblings of the sick kids," I say.

"How do we do this? Just ask each kid what their name is?" Dana asks.

"Yes, let's do it that way. Then when we hear Cielo and Raul, we can pull them aside to talk to them.

"Okay let's all stand outside the bus and ask their names as they go by.

The kids started walking past the four of us and each one gave us their first names. Raul was small for his age as a ten-year-old. Marcos signaled to me and followed him to the plane.

"Raul, can I talk to you a minute?" Marcos asks.

"Sí, qué pasa?" Raul asks.

"Do you know Cielo?"

"Está allí," he says as he points at a girl going up the stairs to the plane.

Marcos signals to Joy and mouths the name Cielo hoping Joy would catch it.

A tall slender teen aged girl of fifteen or sixteen years old stands next to Joy as the others get on the plane.

As I see the worry on her face, I think she wonders if we will let her get on the plane or not. Raul has that same look of fear, like they did something to eliminate them from the group.

I ask Cielo to come down the steps and Marcos tells Raul we need to talk. They both look like they want to cry, but Cielo looks angry.

"Are you going to let me go with the others?" She asks.

"Yes, Cielo. If you want to you can go. There is a problem though. You have a choice. Raul you too."

"What choice?" Raul asks.

"Your little brother and sister are very sick. They are going to go to the hospital as soon as a helicopter arrives. You can choose to go with them to the hospital or get on board with the others."

"What? How sick? Why is she going to the hospital?" Raul asks.

"Tell me how sick my little brother is, please," Cielo says.

"You can see them if you want. They both have high fevers, so the doctor wants them in the hospital as soon as possible. The medicines we carry may not help. He doesn't want to take a chance."

"Let me see my sister!" Raul shouts.

"Yes, I want to see my brother too," Cielo says.

"We can take you to them. We want to make sure you both know you can choose to stay or not. Dana is staying with them. If you stay here, you will be with Dana at the hospital for possibly a few days. Is that something you can do?" I ask.

"I've been in a detention facility, I walked across the desert. I think I can sit in a hospital," Cielo answers.

"I'm sure you can. We also want to make sure you rest and stay healthy. It's not wrong to say you want to get on the plane and rest. Think about it, okay?" I say.

We all walk over to the bus where the two children are resting. We can tell by their eyes they have fever and feel terrible. Raul's sister is about three years old. Cielos's brother is five. They both look like they are burning up from the fever.

"Oh no, pobrecito. Jaime, estás malito?" Cielo asks.

Jaime nods his head and then closes his eyes. Tears run down his cheeks. He thinks he is in trouble too. I can tell.

"Pepa, qué te pasa? Estás malita?" Raul asks.

Pepa can barely nod her head, but by her tears we can tell she just wants Raul to pick her up.

"I'm staying. I can't leave her behind," Raul says.

"Me too, can we both stay?" Cielo asks.

"Of course." Dana answers.

"Ok, the helicopter is landing now. The medics will come over as soon as they land and help load them onto the helicopter. When they are loaded, we will have you get on the chopper with Dana. Okay?" I ask.

"Sí," they both answer.

I wait for the helicopter to land and for the pilot to signal the okay to approach. The two paramedics open the door and jump down. They run to where we are. Each one pulling a stretcher and medical bag.

The noise of the helicopter makes it difficult to hear, but we are able to communicate that the two children have fevers of over 103 and the other two children are siblings who will travel with them. Dana explains he has all of their paperwork as they strap the two smaller children to the stretchers. We all crowd around the children and give the two older ones a hug. Marilyn walks with Dana and the children to the helicopter. As the kids are loaded, I see Dana give Marilyn a huge hug and a kiss. I wish he didn't have to stay behind. How I wish we could all return together.

Marcos, Marilyn and I watch as they close the door of the helicopter. As the blades begin to turn, we see Dana and the two older children waving at us. I hope everything goes well for everyone's sakes. It would be hard for Dana to return without the two sick children, considering he would bring the siblings by himself.

We watch them take off and head back to the plane. It's time for us to get the other forty-six kids to Bear Island Camp. Our attention turns to the task at hand. Marilyn will keep us updated with texts from Dana.

When we board the plane all of the kids are already seated. The doctor requested Gatorade for all of them. Some don't like it but drink it because they are dehydrated. They are offered ginger ale when they finish the Gatorade. We need to keep them hydrated. The sick children are in the back on stretchers and in the arms of nurses. Fewer than twenty kids are sitting up front with Joy.

Marcos walks to the back of the plane to count kids. I count the ones up front. He counts thirty kids in the back who are sick. I count sixteen up front. We have a total of forty-six. The four who left on the helicopter make it fifty. Some of the children in the back are crying, mostly because they are sick. The nurses and the two doctors will be busy on this flight.

The captain asks if we are ready for take-off. I answer that yes, we have forty-six kids and fourteen adults from our group. The attendants already have passed out blankets and pillows to each child. They will try their best to make this the most comfortable flight.

I stand up in front and tell everyone what our plans are.

"Hello everyone, we are glad you are all safe aboard the plane. Some of you are very sick, I know. The doctors and nurses will help you as much as they can. We ask that the group up front stay near us and use the rest rooms up front. We want to reserve the restrooms in the rear for our sickest children."

"¿Adónde vamos? ¿A México?" A child asks.

"No, we are going first to Halifax. It will be a long flight of about six hours. So, get comfortable, eat dinner and watch a movie. You have headphones in the pocket in front of you. If you turn to channel five you can watch in Spanish," I say, but fail to tell them Halifax is in Canada. They don't need to know that right now.

Marcos and Marilyn show them where to find the headphones and how to change the channel of the audio. I wait while they scramble to get plugged in. Maybe it's best to give fewer details this time.

"¿Quíen se montó en el helicoptero?" A boy asks.

"Let me explain to everyone when they have their headphones plugged in," I say.

I tell Marilyn, Marcos and Joy to have them put the headphones down for a minute.

The children look to me and I say, "Two of your friends had a high fever. The doctors wanted them to get the best of care in a hospital. That's why they stayed behind. Raul and Cielo stayed with them. They will catch up to us as soon as they are healthy enough to fly."

The children seem to accept that the others are safe, and they turn back to watch their videos. The plane begins to taxi down the runway after what should have been a two-hour task. The time it took to shower and clean all of the kids was expected, although it did take a little longer than normal, but what set us behind was the time to load the helicopter. We are one hour behind schedule. I ask Joy if I need to let Sam know.

"Of course. He needs to alert the authorities in Halifax that we've had a delay. He'll also tell the staff on Bear Island it may be very late when we arrive. You need to send that text now, I'm sure he's waiting to hear from us," she says.

In a panic I grab my phone and look for Sam's info to text. Joy grabs my arm and says, "Slow down. It's okay. He knows we had to wait for the helicopter. He just needs to know we are in the air. He'll be waiting for your text, but you are doing fine. Take a deep breath, it's good practice to have new experiences each time. No mission is ever going to be the same."

I calm myself and take a deep breath. I begin the text by saying,

'In the air. 46 children aboard, 14 adults. 28 kids are ill and being tended by drs and nurses. Two critical sent to hospital with two siblings. Dana stayed behind to go with them.'

I push send and feel a little better. I want to make sure I do everything Joy would do if she were leading. There is no doubt in my mind Joy has already texted Sam with details.

Marcos asks if I would like to sit with him and the kids. Marilyn is already sitting at the end of one of the rows talking with the kids. I move back to sit with them, and my dinner appears before me. This time it is lasagna and a salad. I love Italian food and realize I'm very hungry. The kids all look at me and laugh. I must look like a wild animal sitting down for a feast.

Bear Island Camp

CHAPTER 12

Marilyn tells us from across the row that Dana sent her a text. "He says the kids are receiving IV antibiotics and they will keep them overnight. The hospital has given the two siblings cots to sleep on and a recliner for Dana. He says they should be fine. Raul and Cielo are a big help with the little ones. He's glad they stayed to help out."

"Good news. I hope they are better by tomorrow to see if they can fly," Marcos says.

"He also says they are being tested for hepatitis. If they have hepatitis they will be held for a longer time," Marilyn says.

"Oh no, let's hope not. We could have a plane full of kids with hepatitis," I say. I finish my meal and think I should have washed my hands before eating. Too late now. We were wearing gloves during the rescue.

I decide to go back to talk with the doctors and nurses. As I approach the first doctor, he looks at me with a smile.

"Doctor, how is everyone? Anyone else have a fever?" I ask.

"Some are running a low-grade fever, but we have given them some Tylenol to help. I think they will be okay. We still have a few vomiting, that may stop when we get off the plane. In the meantime, we are giving them all IV fluids. Some we have given a light sedative to calm them. Why do you ask about the fever?"

"Marilyn just got a text from Dana. The kids in the hospital are on IV antibiotics, but they are also testing them for hepatitis. Do you think our kids here have signs of hepatitis?" I ask.

The other doctor comes over to join the conversation.

"Well, the symptoms of fever, vomiting and diarrhea could be hepatitis. But I didn't notice any jaundice or yellow color in their eyes. It is usually quite obvious. It's possible their status got worse before they got to the hospital. I'm sure the doctors there know what they are doing."

The other doctor agreed, "I don't see any jaundice here with these kids. The vomiting and diarrhea could be from food poisoning, bad water or a stomach bug. I don't believe we have any hepatitis aboard, but we'll check as soon as we get them back to Bear Island. Do doctors come aboard in Halifax? Or just immigration officials?"

"They didn't bring a doctor aboard the last time, but no guarantees they won't this time. Will it be an issue?" I ask.

"They won't want to know we have kids infected with hepatitis, that's for sure. I think the best thing to do is to give the kids as much fluids as possible on the flight. We may have some recuperate enough to sit in the seats. The other ones who are still sick we can give a sleeping aid to sedate them a little, it won't hurt them. They need the rest. That way when they come on board there won't be any crying or screaming from the ones who are sick. I wouldn't mention it. We have passports and visas, right? Just hand them over and act like everything is under control."

"I hate to think they might not let us enter Canada. If they find out, maybe they'll let us through because our only stop is Bear Island. They won't be contagious to anyone else. We can quarantine them if need be when we get to Bear Island. I'll text Sam and let him know what we are planning. Thanks," I say.

More complications. I wonder what Joy thinks. I'm going to go sit with her and discuss the topic to see what her plan would be.

I explain what the doctors have said to Joy. The concern on her face shows it may be a problem. She tells me to text Sam with an update and ask what we should do.

My text to Sam is answered right away. His response says not to worry. He will take care of it. I wonder what he will do. He has no idea if these kids have hepatitis or not, but he doesn't seem to be worried.

A few minutes later a new text comes in, 'Margarita, you have two certified doctors on board and nurses caring for the sick kids. I told them we consider this a rescue mission and we have everything under control. No one will leave the plane in Halifax. You have medical supplies aboard to keep everyone in quarantine if need be. I will let the authorities know that the doctors are convinced it isn't hepatitis and we will conduct testing once we land in Bear Island. Don't worry. It will be okay.'

"Sam says we are a hospital rescue plane and not to worry. They should expect us to carry sick patients. We have two doctors aboard and we are taking precautions. He thinks there is nothing to worry about," I say.

"Sam will take care of it if there is a problem. I know you want this trip to go well. Sometimes it takes a little longer, but it will be okay. If you are worried about getting hepatitis you all had shots. Of course, it depends on what type of hepatitis it is, but you should be fine," Joy says.

"Okay. I trust you and Sam. I know it will work out."

I hope that is true. There is no way I'd like to be contagious to my family or others in Oswego. The kids are waking up and the attendants are serving a snack. Ice cream sandwiches and milk. They all seem very happy to get ice cream. Marcos and Margarita also eat ice cream. When asked I say yes, I'd like one too. Little moments of happiness can come in an ice cream sandwich.

The kids watch Pete the Cat on the big screen. They laugh and eat their ice cream. They look like they don't have a worry in the world. Who would think these kids experienced something so terrible as separation from parent and life in that detention camp? I hope they can soon forget what happened.

The attendants walk through the cabin and pick up trash. They remind us we will be landing in Halifax soon. I'm going to wait before I tell the kids we are leaving the US for Canada. Last time some of the kids got upset. I hope this time it won't be as hard.

Marcos comes over and asks, "How are you doing? Are you worried about immigration?"

"I was, but Sam and Joy reassured me. Sam called and told them we are a hospital rescue plane and they should expect some kids under doctor care aboard. He assures them the doctors don't feel they are contagious, but they are taking all precautions."

"That's good. I want to tell you that Marilyn, Dana and I think you are doing a great job. Me especially. I know how difficult some situations are for you because you had to hide from immigration when you were with your Tío Enrique. But you act so professional. You have been a rockstar!" Marcos says as he gives me a kiss on the cheek.

One of the little boys near us says, "¡Son novios!" He laughs and points at us. The other kids look and smile.

"Es mi marido," I say. He's my husband.

The kids smile and go back to watch their cartoons. Marcos goes back to sit with the kids, and I go back to sit next to Joy.

Joy leans over and says, "It's true, you are doing a great job."

"Thanks, I need a lot of help. I'm so glad you are here, and Sam keeps in touch too."

"Each time gets easier. You'll see. Here, you better grab your envelopes with passports and transit visas. We want to be on the ground as little as possible. We need to get these kids to Bear Island.

The captain comes on and tells attendants to prepare for landing. We are twenty minutes out from Halifax. The attendants walk through the cabin to make sure everyone is buckled in. I stand to look back to see what doctors have decided to do. I see they have some of the sick kids sitting up and buckled in. That leaves less than half of the sick kids still on stretchers with the nurses sitting near them.

As we descend, I realize I haven't told the kids this isn't our final destination today. Is it too late to talk to them now? Should I wait until we land? There will be a few minutes before the cabin door is opened and immigration comes aboard. I'll do it then. Joy looks over at me and smiles and nods her head. I think that means it will all be okay.

A few minutes later we land with a big bump. The kids scream and laugh but relax because we are now on the ground.

While the captain taxis up to where the immigration van is waiting, I decide to brief the kids on what will happen. I stand up and move to the PA system.

"¡Hola! Estamos en Halifax, Canada. Pero no es el destino final."

I watch as some begin to look worried. The questions begin.

"¿Adónde vamos? ¡Quiero ver a mi mamá!"

I know how difficult it is to travel and not know where you are or where you are going. When I traveled by myself on a Greyhound bus from Tijuana to Oregon I didn't know anything about the trip. I was so nervous. These kids have to be very scared. I look to Marcos for reassurance. I hope he will join me in giving the message. Will he or will he think I don't want him to because I'm in charge?

Marcos stands up and says, "Tranquilos, let Margarita finish."

"We will be here for a few minutes and then leave. Immigration will come aboard…"

Some of the kids start to cry, "¡No, la migra no! ¡Quiero a mi mamá!"

"I have passports and visas for all of you. Don't worry. They aren't going to talk to you. They will come through and count how many passengers we have. They want to make sure we have a passport for each one of you. We do. So, don't worry."

"Where are we going?"

"When we leave here, we are going to an island in Canada," I say.

"No, I don't want to go to Canada. I want to go home!" One child says.

"We need to go there because it is safe. We have doctors and nurses there. It will give you time to get healthy. You don't want to go back to that detention center, do you?" I ask.

"¡No!" I hear a no from all of the kids.

"Okay, so please sit quietly while we are on the ground and the immigration people are on board, okay?"

"Sí. Yes, we will be quiet."

I smile and turn around just in time to see the attendants open the door. Within five minutes the immigration officials are climbing the stairs to the plane. Sam probably told them we shouldn't be on the ground for too long.

I stand to greet the officials and hand them the envelope. I tell them we have forty-six children aboard and fourteen adults.

"Here are the passports for each one of the passengers. There is also a transit visa to travel to Bear Island. We departed from Brownsville but never cleared immigration, here is the paperwork," I say as I look at the four officials

Two of them walk down the aisles to count passengers. They both come back and say they have the correct number of passports and visas. The other agent hands me the envelope and says, "Have a safe trip."

Relief sweeps over me. I didn't realize I was holding my breath. I let out a big sigh and I turn and smile at everyone. The agents leave and the attendants close the doors. We decide to let the kids get up and walk around. Some have been up to use the restroom but now they all get up. We ask them to stay in their sections. They can yell back to their siblings if they are awake to see how they are doing. Many conversations fly back and forth across the seats and I can see this relaxes the kids a lot. Maybe we should have done this while inflight. Too late now, it's happening now.

Marcos tells them to do a loop around the seats and even run if they can without knocking each other over. Before we know it there is a line of kids running around the first section of the seats. They are smiling and laughing. They needed to get up and move around.

After everyone has had time to use the restroom and exercise a little, we tell them to start getting settled again. We will take off in ten minutes. I see Marcos is leading the kids running and Marilyn is following the group. The kids in the back watch and clap their hands.

The final loop is made by Marcos leading the first one in line back to his seat. The others follow and find their seats. Marilyn helps them find the seats and get buckled in. What a great team!

The doctors come up front and say, "We may have an issue with one kid. He continues to vomit, and we can't keep any fluids in him. We need to send him to the hospital here. Can we contact the authorities and get an ambulance?"

"Of course, does he have any siblings up front?"

"We don't know but his name is Edgar. Can you ask if anyone is a sibling?"

"Sure, let me check," I say.

I walk forward and ask, "Is anyone here a brother or sister of Edgar?"

No one answers then a young, teenage girl says, "He's my primo. Why?"

"Did you travel with him?" I ask.

"Yes, he lives with us, he is like a brother."

"He is vomiting too much. The doctor wants him to go to the hospital here. One of us will stay with him until he is healthy enough to fly. Do you want to stay with him and go to the hospital? You will still get to join us when he is healthy. It's your choice," I say.

"No, I want to go with him. I need to take care of him," the girl says.

"What is your name?" I ask.

"Tania," she answers.

"Okay Tania, I'm going to introduce you to Marcos and Marilyn if you don't already know them. I lead her over to my teammates and let them know what is happening. I ask them to decide who wants to stay.

I go up to let Joy know we need to ask for an ambulance.

She says, "I'll go ahead and get the ambulance, you let Sam know what is happening. Also let him know who is staying with them."

My text to Sam is short and concise, '*Sam, Joy is ordering an ambulance for one more sick child. We also have a cousin who will stay with him.*'

I pause before sending the text and walk back to see who decided to stay this time.

Marilyn says she will stay. She got to know Tania on the flight and feels comfortable staying with her.

Marilyn pulls me aside and asks, "Do I have to go in a helicopter? I prefer not to."

"No Marilyn, we are in Halifax and there is an ambulance on the way. In Brownsville we had to get a helicopter because we were farther away. We didn't want to take any chances."

I see Marilyn breathe a sigh of relief. What a difference! Dana couldn't wait to get on the helicopter. Marilyn is terrified. I go back to talk with the doctors. I tell them the ambulance is on the way and Edgar's cousin will stay with him. Marilyn will go with them to the hospital.

"Great, we will prepare him for the ambulance. We'll bring him up front now."

"Thanks, they should be here soon," I leave him to help Edgar.

I look out the window and see the ambulance pull up next to the stairway. Two paramedics get a stretcher out and carry it aboard.

Tania stands and says goodbye to the friends she's made on the flight. She grabs Edgar's hand as they take him down the aisle on stretcher. Marilyn gives me a hug and follows the medics down the stairs. I tell her to keep us informed by text.

Now we have forty-four passengers. We started with fifty and we will arrive to Bear Island with only forty-four plus staff. I'm happy we can get that many kids to safety. The rest will follow soon.

The kids are sad to see two more leave the plane. Everything for them is not day to day, but minute to minute. Their lives change and they have no control. Just when they get used to things everything changes and they have to adjust to a new normal.

CHAPTER 13

On our final approach to the airstrip on Bear Island I hear the kid's excitement as they look out over the water and see the lights on the island. They have no idea what is waiting for them here. This place will change their lives forever. Either they will be reunited with family or they will stay on Bear Island and live at the camp until they decide to leave when they are eighteen years old. At that point they will become Canadian citizens. So many opportunities await them.

We descend and land on the airstrip without problems. There are vans waiting for us parked on the runway. They pull closer to the plane once we roll to a stop.

I stand to inform the kids about what is going to happen.

"We are on Bear Island. There are doctors, nurses, teachers and many other helpers here. First thing we need to do is to get you a snack before you go to sleep. When the vans pick up, they'll take us to the camp, and then we'll walk to the lodge for the snack. If anyone needs help walking please let us know," I say

Marcos speaks up, "Let's let the kids in the back off first. If you have a brother or sister there go with them, please."

It is amazing to watch half of the kids fall in behind the wheelchairs and grab the hands of their hermanitos. The rest of the kids seated wait patiently and I wonder if they are here alone. But I look as they move to sit next to their siblings and it's obvious none of them are alone. They were the lucky ones where none of them got sick.

We wait as the nurses and doctors deplane with the kids. Joy waits until everyone is off the plane. She turns to me and says, "Great leadership, Margarita. You had some bumps in the road thrown at you and you dealt with them without hesitation. Great job!" Mary Ellen walks by, smiles and pats me on the back.

"Thanks, Joy. That means a lot. I was worried it would be harder but with your help it went fine," I lean in and give her a hug.

We are the last ones off the plane and the flight crew tell us they will be staying the night in Halifax. They are returning to rest and wait to see if they need to pick up the other kids. We wish them a safe flight and feel the crisp cool air off the island. A big difference from earlier today in Brownsville when it was so hot.

The vans whisk us off to the main camp. The kids are all anxious and asking questions. I think they are very excited because this is a place they've never seen before. An island in the North Atlantic covered in fir trees. They have learned to trust us in the few hours we've spent with them. Marcos and I are so happy to see the smiles on their faces.

When we arrive at the parking lot, we see a crowd of people waiting for us. Like the last time, there is an adult for each child, but this time there are also children with them. I realize they must now be assigned one or two new kids. The kids with them wave and cheer when they see us.

"Margarita and Marcos! Hey, over here! I'm so glad you are back!" I hear some of the kids say. It is nice to see they are so happy and adjusted.

The kids and the adults want to rush forward and hug all of us. The doctors stop them and warn them we need to be tested first. The snack will have to wait. We can get the snack bags and bring them to the medical center. The doctors want to run some tests before uniting the two groups. All of the kids look disappointed, but we tell them it is only temporary. We need to be careful. They walk by the lodge with big eyes and faces filled with disappointment.

The doctors want to rule out hepatitis with the kids who were under doctor and nurse care on the plane. They will test the first group and we will alternate groups.

"Are you tired? I'm excited for the kids but feel worn out. Is that something a mission leader should admit to her team?" I ask Marcos.

"I'm your husband, of course you can say you're are tired. I feel the same way. I feel bad for Dana and Marilyn who are still with kids and aren't back here yet. They must be exhausted," he says.

"Let's get these kids tested. The doctors say they will rush the tests so we should know if anyone has hepatitis within two hours."

"Two hours is a long time when we've been flying all day and night," Marcos answers.

"I know, but as soon as they are tested some of the mentors are going to take over. Joy said we will be able to go sleep in one of the cabins. I can't wait."

The results from the first group comes back within thirty minutes. We are told the first group has tested negative. That was fast. I thought it would take hours. The doctors assured me the lab rushed everything. The first group is clear so they are confident the others will also test negative. Marcos and I are so happy to hear that. None of us wanted to expose the mentors to hepatitis.

Mary Ellen tells us to leave the kids with the doctors and nurses. Mentors will come and pick them up when the testing is done. Marcos and I are so relieved to hear that. We say good-bye to the kids and tell them we'll see them in the morning. We rush over to the cabin we were assigned and settle in for the night. It's not long before we are sound asleep.

The next morning, I am surprised to wake up in a cabin on Bear Island. All night I felt like I was still flying. I hope I don't have to get used to those long flights. Yesterday was a very long day after the long, exhausting night before. We all slept a little on the flight to San Diego, but I never sleep the same on a plane as I do in a bed.

Marcos is already awake and has made coffee. He brings me a cup when I sit up in bed.

"Thanks, I was so tired, but I slept well." I take a sip of coffee and instantly feel better.

"Do you think we should go eat breakfast or sleep longer?" Marcos asks.

"We need to go check on the kids, I think. I wish we could take the day off, but you know we can't. We need to get back to Oswego," I say.

"I'm not sure I even know what day it is, is it still Sunday or did we skip a day?" Marcos asks.

"I think it's Sunday morning, but don't trust me. I'm not quite sure. I hope it's Sunday morning. We left on Friday morning from Oswego and have been flying ever since. It's very tiring, isn't it?"

"For sure, good thing we are young!" Marcos laughs.

We both get dressed and pack our bag. We know we will be flying later today. We leave our things ready to go and walk down to the lodge. When we enter we see that the new group has joined the other kids who were from our first trip. They all shout, "Good morning!" I wish Dana and Marilyn were here and could share this moment with us.

Ricardo and Adriana come up to us to get a hug, "We are so happy you are back." Rosa follows them and gives us a hug.

"Ricardo, how is Memo? I don't see him," Marcos says.

"No, he stays with a nurse in the clinic. They say he's not ready to be with everyone yet. We go visit him every day. He still doesn't talk. They aren't sure what is wrong," he says sadly.

I move in to give Ricardo a hug. "I'm so sorry. This must be so hard for you. I hope they will find a way to help him soon."

"Thanks, I hope so too," Ricardo answers.

I think back to when Ricardo and Memo arrived in the first group. Ricardo was so protective of his little brother. I'm glad they are here together and didn't get separated.

"How long will you stay this time?" Adriana asks.

Marcos turns to Adriana and says, "We'll eat breakfast, check on the kids who arrived last night and then we have to leave. But I hope we can come back soon."

I know that my parents, Sandy, and Junior will be making a trip here soon. I assume Sam may ask us to accompany them. I think he is planning for some time next week. It will be nice to just come for a quick visit and relax. We finish our breakfast and make sure all of the new kids have met up with a mentor and feel safe. We walk over to the medical center to check in on the others. While we are there, we will try to see Memo.

Ricardo walks with us to the medical center. He tells us Memo is still staying there but they are planning on moving him out soon to one of the family cabins.

"Why are they waiting? Is he healthy enough to move?" I ask.

"Yes, but they don't have a family with room yet. It needs to be someone who has time to take care of him during the day, bring him to the medical center and then care for him at night. Right now, he has nurses who are at the medical center 24 hours a day."

"I hope they find someone soon," Marcos says.

When we walk into the medical center, we see some of the kids from the flight last night. The doctors are giving them a final check-up and releasing them to leave with their mentors. They will move to cabins today with their mentors and other kids. It may be a big adjustment, but they all look happy at the moment. The detention center was such a horrible experience, they are excited to be in a happier place.

I see a nurse in the play space set up in the back of the clinic. Memo is on the floor with blocks and other toys. Another child sits near him and jabbers as he plays. He looks up at us, smiles and then waves. Memo looks up but doesn't show any emotion at all. Ricardo goes over and stands him up.

"Remember Margarita and Marcos? They brought us here. We came on the airplane and now we are here on Bear Island. Say hello Memo."

I reach out and pull Memo into a hug. He hugs me back and doesn't want to let go.

I ask him, "How are you Memo? I'm so happy to see you again!"

No reply, but his arms stay wrapped around me. Marcos comes over and pats Memo on the back and says, "Memo, remember me? I'm Marcos."

Memo stays wrapped in my arms and doesn't want to let go.

"Let's walk outside and get some fresh air. Do you want to come outside with me?" I ask.

I start to walk toward the door and Memo walks with me. He doesn't resist and we walk out the front door of the hospital. Marcos looks at me and points at his watch. He knows it's important to spend time with Memo, but he also knows we need to get to the airstrip and get back to Oswego.

An idea pops into my head but it is too outrageous to consider so I don't say a word. Marco looks at me and recognizes the look on my face.

"Okay, what are you thinking?" He asks.

"Maybe he needs a change of scenery. Do you think it would help, Ricardo?" I ask.

"I don't know. They've tried a lot of things here and he still doesn't speak or want to leave the medical center. Today is one of the first days he's been outside."

"Let me give Sam a call." I give Marcos Memo's hand and walk a few feet away to call Sam.

Memo stays still and holds Marcos's hand. His eyes follow me.

When I return, I ask Ricardo a question and he says yes. We both turn to Memo and ask him the same question. He reaches over and takes my hand. He doesn't say yes but doesn't say no either. His only response is when he takes my hand.

Marcos looks at me and says, "Are you sure you want to do this? What are you thinking? We have classes and our work. We can't take care of him. I'd like to say yes but I don't see how it will work.

"The reason I called Sam is to ask when he is sending my parents here. He said as soon as they are ready. Then I asked permission to take Memo and Ricardo to stay with my family before they come here for their visit. Maybe they are the family he needs," I explain.

"Do you think your parents will be open to that? Don't you think you should ask them first?" He asks.

"I already did. They asked how soon we can get the two of them there," I smile.

This idea seemed to fall into place minutes after it popped into my head. We walk back to the medical center and ask the doctor if Memo is okay to travel. He gives his consent and says it might do him good. We pack a bag for him and by the time we leave the medical center Ricardo meets us with his bag packed.

When we meet the van in the parking lot near the lodge Joy doesn't even question what is happening. Her only question is whose idea it was.

"Margarita, is this your idea? Or Marcos was it your idea?" Joy asks.

Marcos speaks up and says, "Joy, you know who it was. Look at Memo. Whose hand is he holding?"

Joy laughs and tells the driver to get us back to the airstrip.

The attendant on the plane says, "You guys are moving kids around all the time. Two more?"

"Yes, they are going back to Oswego with us for a few days. They need a break," I smile.

"No problem, we have lots of room. The captain heard from Marilyn. She is ready for pickup as soon as we return to Halifax," he says.

Ricardo, Memo and Marcos find seats in the center of the plane where they can best see the movie screen. They are ready to settle in for some cartoons. Joy and I are seated up front for take-off. Joy reminds me to check the documents to see if we have everything we need for Ricardo and Memo to enter the US.

I check and start to worry about the visas, but then remember they have transit visas that are still in effect.

"All set, but thanks for the reminder," I say as I lean back in my seat and relax.

I hope this decision will help Memo. My parents will smother him with love and treat him as their own child. They are excited to visit Bear Island and will return in a few days with Memo and Ricardo for their orientation. It just happened to work out.

In comparison to the long flights this weekend, the flight to Halifax seems like it passes by so quickly. I feel bad for Dana and Marilyn who haven't been able to get a full night's rest yet.

Ricardo enjoys getting his meals brought to him and once again asks for a second order of everything. He's a growing boy. Memo eats but doesn't show any excitement. He is still very withdrawn.

When we land in Halifax, I expect the same routine with the immigration officials. When they enter the plane, they are followed by Dana, Marilyn and all of the kids they have chaperoned.

"I'm so happy to see you guys!" I jump up and rush to give them hugs. The immigration officials step back and wait. Marcos and I relax now that our whole team is back together.

The officials check all of the paperwork and we are soon airborne again.

"Wait, we are going to Oswego. You guys are adding extra flying time by going with us," I say.

"Don't worry. We are happy to just be back together. It's lonely when we are split up!" Dana says.

"Why are Ricardo and Memo with you?" Marilyn asks.

"They need a change of pace. They are going to stay with my parents for a few days. Then they'll fly back this weekend with them for their first visit to the island."

"What a good idea!" Marilyn smiles.

We catch up with Marilyn and Dana on the flight and before we know it, we land in Oswego. I hate the thought that they need to turn around and fly back to Bear Island with the kids, but they say they are fine. We say our good-byes and wish them a safe and quick flight. Marcos offers to take Marilyn's place if she wants to rest, but she says she will be fine as long as Dana is with her.

I know Marcos is relieved because he is tired too.

The driver picks us up and asks where we want to go. We tell him to the taqueria, and he turns in the direction toward town.

When we mentioned the taqueria I see Memo look up at me. Ricardo notices too.

"Maybe he remembers when we stopped at a taqueria before we left Baja. We were there with my Papá and Abuelita," he explains.

I have to admit I am very happy to be back in Oswego. As we drive back into town, the places I recognize make me feel at home. Even more when we pull up in front of Francesca's Taqueria. I see Sandy and Junior watching from the front window. They rush out to greet us. They give Ricardo and Memo a big hug. I see Memo's face light up when he walks into the taqueria.

Bear Island Camp

CHAPTER 14

My parents rush over to hug us.

My mother takes one look at Memo and says to him, "¿Hijo, te puedo dar un abrazo?"

She doesn't wait for him to respond and moves in to give him a motherly hug. He lets her hug him and stays wrapped in her arms for a long time. Ricardo watches and I see a tear in his eye. My mom looks over and pulls him into a hug with Memo.

My dad waits until the hugs are over, then stretches his hand out to Ricardo to shake his hand. He does the same to Memo. Memo doesn't take his hand but does look up at him.

We all sit down at a big table and Sandy and Junior bring us drinks, chips and salsa and guacamole. I realize I'm hungry and can't wait for some of my mother's homemade tortillas.

My dad runs into the kitchen to cook us some food. When my mom gets up to help, Memo says, "Teresa."

"What?" Ricardo asks. "Qué dices Memo?"

"Teresa," he repeats as he points to my mother.

It's the first time he's spoken since the detention camp. Ricardo is shocked. Marcos and I both look over to Ricardo and then to Memo.

"Why do you think he said Teresa? Is that your mother's name?" Marcos asks.

"No, it's her friend. We stopped in a taqueria. They owned the taco shop. We ate there and they were very kind to us. Memo knows she was a my mother's friend. Maybe he thinks you are Teresa's friend and you will know Mamá."

"Well, let's try to keep him talking if possible. We won't force him but encourage him. This is a time of celebration. Memo is speaking. Or at least he said one word.

When Mamá puts a plate of tortillas on the table Memo says, "Mamá. Las tortillas de Mamá."

Although it's sad we all smile. He remembers his Mamá and her friend Teresa. That's progress.

When the food is placed in front of us Memo smiles and says, "Jamaica, agua de Jamaica."

"¿Quieres agua de Jamaica, hijo? Te voy a traer some hibiscus flower punch," My mom says as she rushes to the kitchen.

We are all astonished that Memo is speaking. I think the most surprised is Ricardo. He has been so sad on Bear Island because Memo was incommunicative. Ricardo is smiling and looks at me and says, "Thank you for this. He just needed a taqueria and someone who he thinks is a friend of our mother."

"It was a risk, just an idea I had. I'm glad it worked," I say.

Mamá returns to the table with a pitcher of agua de jamaica. Memo turns and looks at Ricardo and laughs. It's amazing what memories help to bring him out of his depression or whatever he had.

When we finish breakfast, Junior asks Memo if he would like to go to the park to play. Memo nods his head yes, but then looks at Ricardo to see if it's okay. Ricardo says yes, then looks at me to make sure.

"Of course, that's a good idea Junior. Take Memo down to the playground. But only for an hour, we don't want him to get overtired, this is his first day out playing," I smile.

Sandy looks at Ricardo and says, "Do you want to meet some of my friends? I was going to go to my friend's house."

Ricardo turns to Marcos and whispers something in his ear. I look to Marcos to see what the problem is. Marcos smiles and says, "Ricardo if anyone asks you where you came from just say you are visiting from Canada. You live in Canada for now. They won't ask anything else. If anyone asks about Memo just tell them he has been sick. You are here visiting family."

"Yes, that's a perfect answer. Sandy, did you hear what Marcos said? You know how we couldn't always tell everyone about where we were from? That's what it's like for Ricardo and Memo right now. They are just here visiting, okay?"

"Yes, of course. I get it. Let's go Ricardo. We'll be back in an hour. Memo will want to know where Ricardo is when he gets back, I think."

"Perfect, have fun!" Mamá says.

As they leave, we all sit back down and give a sigh of relief.

"Hija, I'm so glad you thought of this. What made you think of it?" Papá asks.

"I just remembered when we were on the ship and the agents wanted to separate us. Remember none of us wanted to separate. Marcos and I got married. Yasmene and Miguel got married just so we could stay together as a family. I know that decision really helped us all to heal from our past traumas. Well, I thought maybe what Memo needed was to feel like he's part of a family. Since you are moving to Bear Island, I thought of you," I explain.

"I think it worked," my mamá says.

"What about when we go to Bear Island? Will they stay with us or go back to live with others?" Papá asks.

"It depends what you want to do. Do you want them to live with you? They have been looking for a family or mentor for them. They couldn't find anyone who had enough time to care for Memo. It looks like he won't need as much care. You have Junior and Sandy who can help," I say. I hope they will consider keeping them.

"We know what it was like when you got separated from us. We are thankful to all of the people who took care of you. Why would we say no? It's obvious they need a family. Do they know if they will ever be able to return to their family? I know his mother is dead, but what about their father?"

Marcos explains, "They haven't been able to find their father or abuelita. Sam tries every way he can to find them. When they can't, they try to find them a family or mentor who will take them in as family. He tries to give them a permanent situation."

"It may be early for them to make a decision but I think they feel left out. The other kids have moved in with their mentors. I know they will be so happy to hear the news. Do you want to tell them? I'll check with Sam first, but I don't think there will be a problem," I say.

"We'll wait for you to let us know. In the meantime, we'll plan on them living with us as family. I look forward to having them with us!" My mamá says.

We all sit around smiling at the table. We hardly realize an hour has passed when Memo runs in and shouts,"¿Ricardo? Dónde estás?" He looks around and then his face crumbles into a pout that we all know will turn into a cry.

"Memo, he'll be right back. He went with Sandy to see a friend. He'll be back any minute," I say.

"Junior and Memo, do you want some ice cream?" Papá asks.

Memo turns to look at Papá and asks, "¿Chocolate?"

"Of course! Do you want chocolate? We'll have chocolate. How about you Junior?" He asks.

"Chocolate of course, I want what Memo wants," Junior answers.

With the promise of chocolate ice cream Memo forgets about Ricardo.

The boys are seated in a booth and talking. The chocolate ice cream and the trip to the park has made them fast friends. Memo has returned to being a kid. I call Sam and let him know we are doing well. Memo and Ricardo have settled in. I ask him about my parents taking them in to live with them once they are all on the island.

"Margarita, that is such great news. We have been so worried about Memo and Ricardo. Memo was on our list of critically depressed. We were worried about Ricardo because he was so concerned about Memo. We expected him to crash at some point. I think you have turned this around and they may be out of danger. There is only one problem," he says.

"What is that?'

"If we find their family, we may have to send them back home. Are your parents prepared for that? Make sure they understand the situation," Sam answers.

"I'm glad you reminded me. I will let them know that it's a possibility," I say.

"Yes, now go home. You and Marcos need to get some rest. Great job! Go home!" He says with emphasis on home.

"We will. Thanks for your help. Oh, by the way. Have you heard from Marilyn and Dana yet?" I ask.

"I think they are on their way to Bear Island. We haven't heard from them since take off."

"Anything to be concerned about?" I ask.

"No, I'm sure it's nothing. Go home and rest. We'll let you know tomorrow. They will probably be back in Oswego by then. Good night," Sam says.

"Good night, Sam," I say as I click off the call. I am worried now. Why haven't Dana and Marilyn touched base with Sam? Should I tell Marcos or keep it to myself?

I pull my mother and father away from the group and tell them what Sam said. "Sam loves the idea of Ricardo and Memo living with you on Bear Island. But he wants me to remind you if their father or abuelita are found and ask for them back you will have to return them. Are you prepared for that?"

"Well, that would be very difficult. What are the possibilities of finding them?" Mamá asks.

"We have only returned six of the fifty kids from the first group. They were separated at the border and may not have found each other. That's why it's important to try to help them." I say.

"We will treat them as family. If the opportunity for them to return to their family comes up, we will of course make that happen. We know how we felt when we were separated from you Margarita. We wouldn't want to rob anyone of getting their kids back. Don't worry about us. They will always be family whether they continue to live with us or not. Should we ask them now?" My papá asks.

Just as he says that Sandy and Ricardo come through the door.

"Perfect timing!" I say.

"Let's all sit down for a few minutes. Marcos and I have to get home for some rest. We have classes tomorrow," I say.

All of the kids look at us because the mood has changed, and the adults look very serious. My parents stand up and hold hands as they look at Ricardo and Memo.

"Boys, we would like to invite you to live with us on Bear Island. We are moving there soon and would love it if you were part of our family. What do you think?" Papá says.

Memo and Ricardo look at each other. Ricardo starts to say something to Memo, but Memo stops him.

"I know Mamá died. I heard one of the nurses in the medical center talking. I've known for a long time," he says.

"Memo, I didn't tell you because you were so weak. Believe me I wanted to tell you when we were still in Mexico but Papá said no. He thought you were too young to understand," Ricardo says.

"I know. Will Papá look for us? Where is Abuelita?" He asks.

Marcos decides to step in,"The people we work for will continue to look for your Papá and your Abuelita. But so far, they haven't found them. It's very difficult to locate people once immigration picks them up, but we're not giving up. If they find them, we will put you in contact with them and help you reconnect."

Mamá says, "I know I can never replace your mamá, but you need someone right now. Will you let me be your Mamá until they find your family?"

Papá says, "I can be your Papá until they find your real father. Will you let me be your Papá?"

Ricardo takes Memos hand and says, "What do you think Memo? I say yes. What about you?"

"Sí, I agree," Memo answers.

We are so used to the group hug that Sandy started on board the ship that we don't even wait for her to say it, but she does, "Group hug!"

CHAPTER 15

When Marcos and I arrive home we are too exhausted to think about anything. We go to sleep right away. The next morning while making coffee I get a text from Yasmene.

The text reads, '*Miguel and I would like to get together with you and Marcos tonight. Do you want to come to dinner?*'

I want to say no because we are exhausted, but we haven't seen them in a week or two. I miss them.

Of course, what time? I answer.

'*Six would be great! Can't wait to see you two!*' Yasmene answers and adds a heart emoji.

I let Marcos know about dinner when he comes into the kitchen. By the look on his face I can see he wants a night at home just like I do. He doesn't say it, but I know that face. It's a face of exhaustion and tiredness of being around other people. He likes alone time and I do too. We are almost at our limit.

He says okay and then adds, "Can we take this morning off from running? I'm exhausted."

I agree as I hand him his coffee. We stand at the counter and drink our coffee and stare into space. Neither one of us wants to break the silence.

"I need some alone time, do you?" he asks.

"Yes, I just want to sit quietly for a while. What do you want to do?" I ask.

He laughs and says, "I think I'm going to take a nap. To be honest this is wearing me out. We have another trip back to Bear Island this weekend. If we had to fly another mission to Texas and back, I think I'd have to say no. It's going to be hard to say no to Sam."

"He knows how tiring it is. I hope he gives us a break too. This weekend will be a family trip. Not as stressful. Mamá and Papá will take care of Ricardo and Memo. We will just be riding along I hope," I sigh.

"I'm going back to bed," Marcos leans in and gives me a kiss and takes his coffee to the bedroom.

"Wait, I'm going to grab my pillow and blanket and crash on the sofa," I say quickly.

As we both settle in for some alone time I glance at my phone. I don't want to turn it off, but I do turn the volume down.

The next thing I know Marcos is shaking me awake, "Margarita, we overslept. We missed class."

"You know I don't care right now. We needed to sleep and not be around people. I think Professor Ricks will understand. I'm not sure about my math professor, but we can't keep up this schedule and go to class the day after we get home, it's insane."

Marcos sits down next to me, "I know. It's the first time I don't care about school. Our work is tiring but it's so important. We can go to class anytime, but it's not any day we can help fifty kids get out of a detention camp."

"I agree. I'm still exhausted though. Do you want to stay home or go to the taqueria to eat?" I ask.

"That's an easy question to answer. I want to do both," he says.

"We could go and get a carry out, but that might seem rude to my family. Ricardo and Memo might want us to stay."

"Let's think on it a minute. I don't need to eat yet, do you?" He asks.

"No, not hungry yet. Let's watch some TV and decide later," I say.

We stare mindlessly at a rerun of Jeopardy and neither says a word for the whole show. Unusual for us because we like to shout out the answers we know. Not today. I am just worn out.

"Let's stay home and eat, I don't have the energy to walk downtown," Marcos says.

"I can make us breakfast. Do you want some eggs?" I ask.

"Perfect! Eggs would be perfect," Marcos laughs.

I go to the kitchen and realize we haven't heard from Dana or Marilyn. I check my phone and see I have multiple texts from both of them. I read through them and forget about making breakfast.

"Marcos! Dana is sick. Marilyn and Dana texted me, but my phone was turned down. I didn't hear the texts come in," I call from the kitchen.

"What? Where is he? Do we need to go help?" Marcos asks.

"Let me call Marilyn. Hold on," I say.

"Marilyn, how are you? Where are you? I'm sorry my phone was turned down," I say with worry in my voice. How could I have been so selfish to turn my phone off?

"We are in a hospital in Halifax. Dana got really sick and his symptoms seemed to mimic what the kids had. High temperature, stomach issues and diarrhea. He wasn't feeling well when we saw you on the flight back to Oswego. He didn't want to say anything because he knew you were both tired. On the flight from Oswego to Halifax he got sicker. His temperature was 103 and the attendant told the captain. He landed us in Halifax and had an ambulance meet us at the airport. They rushed him to the hospital. I'm here with the kids, trying to keep them calm. The younger ones are hard to handle now. They've been traveling for days."

By now I have the call on speaker phone so Marcos can hear too. We both know what we need to do.

"We are going to call Sam and check in to see if we can get a flight to Halifax. We'll come and trade places with you," I say.

"I know you both just got home and are still exhausted. But I'm not sure how much longer I can hang in there," I hear Marilyn's voice crack.

"We'll call you right back. Don't worry about us," Marcos says.

We call Sam and first get to speak with Mary Ellen. She is happy to hear from us, but I can hear the worry in her voice.

"Mary Ellen, we were sleeping and didn't hear any of the texts until now. Can we go help Marilyn? They need to get back here as soon as they can. They are both exhausted," I say.

"Well, Sam is hoping you can help out. Joy is still laid up and may have a virus, too. If you two are healthy and willing to go, we can get it organized," Mary Ellen says.

"I have an idea that may help everyone. What if we move up my family's visit to Bear Island and they go with us?" I ask.

"I think it's too much. Dana and Marilyn need to get back asap. If you go to Halifax, you can pick up the kids and take them to Bear Island. On the way back the plane can land again in Halifax and pick up Marilyn and Dana. They need to rest, and Dana hasn't been released from the hospital yet.

"Let's get you two to Halifax first. Sam and I both know you are exhausted but grateful you can go and help them. Let your professors know you are out due to a family emergency," she says.

"Okay, I need to let my parents know too and cancel a dinner for tonight. What time do you think we can leave?" I ask.

"As soon as Sam has the details, we will call you. But the sooner the better; you can stop by here and get new uniforms if you don't have clean laundry. We can do that for you," Mary Ellen says.

"Okay, we'll get our go bag ready. If we need uniforms, we'll let you know," I say as I see Marcos dump our laundry into the washer and set the quick wash option. If we have time to get our laundry dry, we won't have to stop at Home Base. That will save time.

Marcos runs around grabbing our toothbrushes and necessary items we just unpacked last night. The exhaustion we both felt earlier disappears and we feel an urgency to get to Halifax. I send a text to Yasmene to let her know we have to cancel dinner tonight. '*Something came up'.* I start to put the phone down and hear a text come through.

'What is so important you can't come to dinner? You need to come to dinner!'

I wonder if they have signed the NDA with Sam yet. What if they decide to not join up and go to Bear Island this summer?

I decide to call Yasmene. She answers right away and says, "Really Margarita, what is so important you can't come over to dinner. Miguel and I really need to talk to you."

"Have you been contacted by Joy or Sam Mason? They said they would contact you while we were away."

"Yes, what have you gotten us into? Miguel and I aren't sure we can join you. It's all too mysterious. Joy came to our apartment and tried to say because you all are working for them that we have to join. We like to talk things over first," she says without taking a breath.

"I understand your hesitancy. I felt the same way when they first recruited me. Did they give you all of the details?" I ask.

"I'm not sure what details could change our minds. You already have your parents and family involved. We wish you would have talked to us as a group. We are part of this family too!"

Now I understand where I messed up. I didn't include them in the meeting with my parents. I should have done that. Sam asked me not to was one reason, but I should have known better. Yasmene and Miguel are just as important as anyone else in this family.

"I apologize, I should have included you guys in our meeting. I did think it would have been easier, but Sam wanted to make sure it would work out for them first."

"That's the other thing, they agreed and didn't consider they would be leaving us here alone in Oswego. You all will move to Bear Island and we'll be here without family."

"No, that's not how it will work. Marcos and I will remain here and finish our studies. We will go for the summer. Sam would like you two to go and live there for the summer too. You can come back in the fall and continue your studies too."

"What about work, Margarita? I work and so does Miguel."

"Did they explain the financial portion of the deal? It doesn't sound like it," I say.

To make this happen I need to be the person passing the info on to them. If Joy or Sam didn't get that far it must be that they didn't think they were going to sign the NDA.

"Okay, did you sign an NDA with Joy?" I ask.

"No, we didn't want to because it seemed so strange."

"That's why they didn't explain more to you. Do you have time to listen for five minutes? I can explain more."

"Yes, but I'm not sure it'll change my mind."

"Okay, do you have to do an internship or work shadow to get your nursing license? I know you work at the hospital now. Does that count toward hours of practicum?" I ask.

"No, it doesn't count. I have to do so many hours in another facility. It can't be here where I work," she says.

"Perfect, you can complete your hours in the medical center on Bear Island if you go this summer."

"If I quit my job for the summer, I have to wait to get rehired again. I can't just quit," she says.

"Hold on a minute and I'll explain how you can. Does Miguel need to do student teaching in a school?"

"Yes, that's why I can't quit my job. While he is teaching, he can't work in the same school. He has to take a semester off. We need my salary for that semester."

"Sam has a solution. If you promise you'll think about signing the NDA I can fill you in. Will you think about it?" I ask.

"Yes," she says.

"Okay, first of all any time you work for Sam you get paid. Any training, travel or time. He pays for everything. He also pays for your tuition if you work for him."

"What, how does he do that?" She asks.

"He's a billionaire. He uses his money to help others. He recruits people like us to help others in the world. He's a good person. It's not a cult." I assure her.

"When we go to visit Bear Island this weekend you should come with us. It's a beautiful place. There is a medical center where they need your help. You'll be able to get your practicum done and Sam will find a professor or professional who will sign off, so you get your credits and experience. There is a school and they need Miguel.

He can do his student teaching there and get his paperwork signed too. Sam will make sure of that."

"Really?"

"They have great daycare while you two work. You will also get your own family cabin to live in. You will live in a community but have your own privacy. Mamá, Papá, Sandy and Junior will live nearby."

I consider telling her about Ricardo and Memo but think it might be too much information right now.

"Can you think about joining us this weekend please? If you sign the NDA, we can all go as a family this weekend. It will be like a mini vacation."

"Let me talk to Miguel. He's still at work. So, you can't come tonight?" She asks.

"No, I can only share that we will be helping bring home some sick friends. After the NDA is signed, I can share so much more information. I have already told you too much. But please I hope you can come with the whole family this weekend. It will mean so much to everyone that we are all there."

"I think I can convince Miguel, but I need to go get ready for work. When will you be back from this trip? I miss you. We haven't seen you in a long time," Yasmene says.

"I know. It has been hard to find time. When we are home, we have to catch up on homework and sleep. I'll let you know as soon as we get back. In the meantime, stop by the taqueria if you want to hear how they feel about Bear Island. They have a surprise to share," I say.

"You can't tell me? You are so mysterious, but we'll try to stop there tonight since you can't come to dinner. Maybe you should come up with a code word for things you can't share, like pineapple or something," she laughs.

"How about we keep that word? Pineapple ,.,

Sounds good to me," I laugh. "It's not top secret but I prefer Mamá and Papá tell you. They will be so excited to share their news. I'm surprised they haven't called you, but they are very busy," I say.

"Okay, pineapple it is. Talk to you soon," she says.

"Bye Yasmene, I'm so glad we got to talk. I feel so much better now. I would never want you to be upset with me," I say.

Marcos comes into the kitchen as I put my phone down. "How is Yasmene?" he asks.

"Oh, better now. They were upset with us. But I explained as much as I could without giving everything away."

"Why can't you tell them everything? Aren't they going to work for Sam?" he asks.

"They had a lot of questions and didn't sign the NDA yet. They thought we made too many family decisions without including them. I explained it will all make sense soon. They still didn't know that Sam would pay them and pay their expenses. They were worried about quitting their jobs. Now they understand it a little bit better," I answer

"Our clothes are in the dryer. I hope we can get our clothes dry before Sam calls back," Marcos says as he brings our two go bags to the kitchen.

"Thanks, that will be better if we don't have to stop at Home Base," I say. "I can make us a sandwich or some food to take with us. What do you think?'

"I'll have a bagel and coffee. I think we'll have time to eat on the plane. We won't have much else to do except nap,"

"That's true. I'll get that ready. Go relax a bit. Sam should call soon," I say.

We have time to eat our bagel and have a second cup of coffee before Sam calls back. Our clothes are dry and packed. Marcos starts to get anxious and wants me to call Sam or Mary Ellen. I tell him to relax, they will call whenever everything is ready. He grabs his backpack to look through work he missed in today's class. We are both ready to go and don't want to wait any longer. We need to go help Marilyn. Dana is in good hands at the hospital, but Marilyn is supervising six kids and is exhausted. We feel useless sitting here while she is still working and exhausted.

Sam calls and tells us everything is in motion. A car will pick us up in fifteen minutes. He asks if we need to stop by Home Base. I tell him we are ready to leave, we have everything we need. He tells me he'll send our weapons with the driver; he doesn't feel we'll need them but thinks we should have access to them at all times.

I don't think we will need them crossing into Canada, but he feels when we are transporting kids, we need to have protection at all times. He tells me I'm in charge.

"But Sam, this is just Marcos and I. Dana and Marilyn are friends, we are just going to help out. It's not really a mission is it?" I ask.

"Yes, it is. You are transporting kids that haven't reached Bear Island yet. I need someone to make decisions and handle any issues that come up. Are you up for it?" He asks.

"Yes, I understand, don't worry," I say.

"Good, thanks to you and Marcos for doing this. We know how tired you are. This is above and beyond. Try to sleep on the plane, okay? Take care!" And Sam clicks off of the call.

Marcos looks at my face and says, "Okay, what? What did he say? I can tell he said something you don't want to tell me."

"He put me in charge again," I say.

"That makes sense, why does that bother you?" Marcos asks.

"I guess someone has to be in charge Last time Joy was with us and we had fifty kids. Now it's just the four of us and four kids. He says as long as we are still transporting kids, we need to have someone in charge. I just don't like to tell you guys what to do," I say.

"Why not? It'll be fine. Don't worry about it. What can go wrong? We fly to Halifax and pick up the kids. We transport them to Bear Island and then return for Marilyn and Dana. It's not a difficult mission," Marcos assures me.

"The car will be here in a few minutes. He's also sending the weapons case. He says as long as we are transporting kids we need to be armed. That surprised me."

"Makes sense, he's just being extra careful. Don't worry, we've got this," he says and gives me a hug.

I remember to call my parents and tell them we are on another work trip. I also mention that Yasmene and Miguel will stop by for dinner tonight. I let them know I didn't tell them about Ricardo and Memo.

She asks what kind of work trip and I tell her Dana is sick and we need to help out. He'll be fine but he and Marilyn need our help to transport the kids with them. We should be back by tomorrow evening at the latest. It is so much nicer to be able to let them know what we are doing instead of making up lies.

Marcos and I board the small plane to Halifax and hope our trip will be easy and uneventful.

Bear Island Camp

CHAPTER 16

Our arrival in Halifax seems too quick. Sam has a car waiting for us and it zooms us to the terminal where we easily move through customs. Our plane will wait here while we go to the hospital to pick up the kids.

We aren't used to going through airports. Since we started working for Sam we always pass through customs and immigration on the runway waiting for take-off. Today seems like more work as we need to make our way through the crowds. Halifax isn't a huge airport but big enough for us to stick together. We don't want to get separated.

When we finally make it to the curb there is a driver with a sign saying Margarita and Marcos. We laugh and wave at the driver. We jump into the car and he knows we want to go to the hospital right away. He makes small talk but must know not to ask too many questions. Our military-style uniforms with black cargo pants and polo shirts are received with surprised looks and respect. People don't recognize the Bear Island insignia and wonder who we are. We are very young to get such VIP treatment.

We arrive at the hospital in only a few minutes. I text Marilyn to let her know we are here. By the time we enter the hospital doors we see Marilyn walking toward us carrying one child and holding hands with another one. Two older ones follow behind her with two siblings in tow. She looks exhausted.

Marcos reaches in to get the child she is holding and takes the hand of the other little one. Marilyn gives me a huge hug and whispers in my ear, "I'm so tired, these kids never stop. I don't know if I ever will be a mother. It's so much work."

"We are so glad we can help. Sorry this happened. Next time we need to make sure we take turns staying behind when we need a volunteer. Promise me that," I say.

"I promise, no arguments here," she says.

"We want to go up to see Dana before we leave, what room is he in?" Marcos asks.

"I'll go with you. I know this place so well. We've taken so many walks up and down these hallways. They know us in the cafeteria so well. This morning we were in the cafeteria the minute they opened. The staff has been so great with food and the nursing staff helped with diapers and clean t-shirts. I hope they can get these clothes off soon," Marilyn says.

"We brought them clothes too. Sam sent a bag. He also sent clean clothes for you and Dana," I say.

Her smile shows me how appreciative she is. It's been a long few days for her. We walk down the hall and the two older kids run ahead to show us where Dana is. Marilyn looks like a mother duck with her ducklings.

Dana smiles when he sees us. He wants to get up, but Marilyn tells him to stay in bed until the doctor comes in. He salutes her with his right hand and says, "Yes, ma'am."

"I follow Marilyn's orders more than the doctors and nurses. She's been taking care of me and the kids. She sure needs a break. I'm so glad you are here," Dana says.

I leave Marcos to talk to Dana and I take the three older kids into the bathroom and show them the fresh bag of clothes. I realize since they are a girl and a boy, I need to leave one at a time to change. I grab the second set of clothes and walk the young girl down the hall to the public restroom. When we return Marilyn has the two younger children changed and outfitted in a clean set of clothes. She looks so eager for this to be the last time she has to change their clothes.

Dana smiles at me and says he is so glad we all work together. I agree with him. It is more fun to work with friends.

The doctor comes in and sees all of us. He smiles and says, "The cavalry has arrived to help out?"

We say, "Yes, we are here to take the kids,"

He says, "Dana is well enough to travel if we want to wait for his discharge papers."

"Well, we could, or we could come back and pick you up," I say to Dana and Marilyn.

Dana jumps up out of bed and says, "No, I'm going with you. I don't want to stay another minute in the hospital."

We laugh and Marcos says, "You could leave the hospital and go out to lunch or visit Halifax. You don't have to leave with us."

Marilyn looks at us and says, "I have no desire to be a tourist. I'm getting on the plane with you!" Dana agrees with her.

Within the hour Dana has his medications, we have the children and we walk out of the hospital. Marcos texted Sam and we have a van waiting for us at the front door with car seats and a driver. It's amazing what Sam can do from Home Base. He must have so many connections around the world.

On the drive to the airport one of the kids asks if we are returning to Mexico. I look over at her and answer, "Not yet. First, we are going to a safe place. There'll be a place for you to live and you'll be taken care of."

"Will Marilyn take care of us? I want to stay with Marilyn," she says.

The other child agrees, "Yes, I want Marilyn to stay with us."

Marilyn looks over at them and says, "Let's get to Bear Island first. I might not be able to stay, but I'll make sure you are safe with someone. I'll be back to visit for sure."

She turns away and I see a tear roll down her cheek. During this short time together the kids and Marilyn have bonded. It will be hard for her to leave them even though she says she is exhausted.

Even though the plane is waiting on the runway we need to walk through the airport again. This time with the kids I have all of the passports and there shouldn't be a problem. It makes me nervous, but I know we have the correct paperwork.

Dana wants to stop and get some ice cream. He says he got used to eating ice cream in the hospital and knows it won't make him sick. He buys ice cream for everyone. We must look very strange walking through the airport. There is Dana, a tall blonde guy, two Mexican adults with sidearms, a Chinese woman and, six Mexican children. All with an ice cream cones in their hand. We rush to the gate because we want to leave as soon as possible. We are dressed in our uniforms and the kids in shorts and t-shirts with Bear Island Camp written on them. People have to be curious, but no one asks us anything.

We near the gate and see our attendants we know so well waiting for us. They wave and smile. We are happy to see them. Now it is up to them to take care of us until we land once again.

Once aboard the plane, we buckle the kids in and place one of us sitting next to them in every other seat. I tell Dana and Marilyn to go sit by themselves and rest, but they don't listen and settle in.

I try to distract the kids. This small plane doesn't have the large screen tv, but it does have smaller ones. I give each of the older kids headphones and show them how to turn them on. I can see why Marilyn is exhausted, she not only had to take care of them she got very close to them. I understand because that's how Marcos and I feel about Ricardo and Memo.

Our flight is easy and within two hours we are landing on Bear Island. The van is waiting to take us to the parking lot and lodge. The kids are amazed the trip is finally over. We explain to them that the kids they started the trip with are here already.

There is a welcoming party in front of the lodge when we pull up. One of the doctors, a nurse and two mentors wait for us. The doctor tells us to be on the safe side we need to take them to the medical center first. We agree it's for the best.

One of the girls grabs Marilyn's hand when she sees there are other adults who want to take them. Marilyn doesn't let go but I can now see it's going to be a difficult good-bye. She walks ahead with the kids.

I pull the doctor to the side, "We need to get them settled with their mentor soon. They are very attached to

Marilyn and she is exhausted. When we leave, they aren't going to be happy. Do you have someone in mind who can step in?"

"We have it under control. We have the exact person who can help. She's new and hasn't been assigned anyone yet. We'll get her over here right now. Don't worry Margarita. These kids will be so distracted they will say good-bye without a tear," he says.

I hope so, I think to myself.

Dana follows Marilyn but I can tell he needs to rest. I try to tell him to go to the lodge and get some coffee or food. His response is he is staying until Marilyn is ready to say good-bye to the kids. He knows it's going to be emotional and he wants to be there.

While the doctor and nurse check the kids out, I see a young woman bounce into the medical center. She literally bounced in. She is a tall, Samoan young woman with an infectious smile. She looks at us and says, "Where are my kids? I can't wait to meet them."

We introduce ourselves and find out her name is Lulu. She is just the right person to take over the kids from Marilyn. The kids will love her.

"But wait, are you going to mentor all of the kids? There are too many for one mentor," I say.

"Sam thought it would be okay since my husband is here too. These kids have been together during the trip and he wants to keep them together. They'll live with us at our house," she says.

Just then a tall muscular Samoan young man runs up the steps and comes into the medical center. Sam is right, these two are the perfect couple.

Rangi introduces himself, and says he has heard so much about us. He's very happy he and his wife can help with these kids who just arrived.

"We've been waiting to meet the kids assigned to us," Rangi says.

Dana speaks up and says, "You two are exactly what these kids need. They've connected with Marilyn and I and we are feeling bad we can't stay with them. Let's introduce you to them."

"Okay, let's do it!" Lulu says.

We lead them back to where the kids are sitting with one of the nurses. They're all checked out and can now start their life here at Bear Island

When we walk in Lulu says, "Hello everyone! I'm Lulu. What are your names?"

The kids look at her in awe and smile. Rangi follows up with, "I'm Rangi! Who wants to come to play on the playground? We have a special fort that's just been finished. I think we need to find a name for it. Who wants to come with Lulu and I to go see it?"

Two kids raise their hands. The little ones are too young to be able to answer or know what a fort is. "Me, I want to go. Marilyn can we go with them?" Raul asks while he looks up to Marilyn. Cielo says she will go but is a bit old for a fort.

"Sure, go ahead and have fun! Lulu and Rangi will take you. Later they'll bring you to the lodge to see us, okay?" Marilyn says.

Dana says, "Wish I could go to the playground with you, but I need to go with Marilyn."

We all watch as Lulu and Rangi take the kids down the path to the playground. I think we all want them to bond with those two in the next fifteen minutes. Maybe they will have so much fun they will forget that Marilyn and Dana are leaving.

We walk up to the lodge and say hello to everyone there. We grab a snack and find a place to sit by ourselves. Many of the kids stop by to say hello while we eat our quick lunch.

"How do you think the kids will do with Lulu and Rangi? Do you think they'll be okay with saying good-bye?" Marilyn asks.

"Yes, I think they will be fine, but how will you be?" I ask.

"I'm fine but I'm so exhausted I might get emotional. Can you guys help me if I do? Please get us out of here if I start to cry," Marilyn says.

"Don't worry Marilyn, we've got your back. Let's hope they come soon. I want to get home tonight," Dana says.

"Let me give the medical center a call. Maybe someone can go out and find them," I say.

"No, wait, let's send one of the kids here. They are busy at the medical center," Marcos says. He calls kids over and asks if they know Lulu and Rangi. They nod their heads and smile, "Yes, they are so much fun. They are new."

"Can you go find them please and ask them to come here?" He asks.

"Sure," and two of them head out to find Lulu and Rangi.

No sooner had they left the door than they came back in with the smiling group. They come over to us and sit down with us. We can tell they are happy because everyone is smiling and laughing. They didn't even try to sit next to Marilyn which is a relief for her.

One of the kids says, "We have a cabin, each one of us has a bunkbed and our own toys. Even my little brother has his own crib. It's prefect for us."

Cielo says, "It's almost like they knew us before we arrived. It's just the right size for everyone. We have the whole loft to ourselves. It has a ladder to climb up to our beds. We are going to have so much fun."

Marilyn says, "That makes me so happy. I'm so glad you like it here. I have to go back home now. Dana too. You will be safe and happy here with Rangi and Lulu."

The children look sad for a moment and one whispers in my ear, "Is Marilyn going to be okay?"

I whisper back, "Yes, she will be fine. We all will be. Marcos and I will be back this weekend with some other new people. We'll see you then okay?"

"Yes," and she stands up to give Marilyn a hug, then Dana. They did bond with them but now feel safe here because of the great welcome and home that has been made for them.

Marcos signals that it's time to get going by coughing and making a hand signal like an airplane. We get up and make our way to the door. They wave good-bye to us as well as the other kids in the lodge. We need to move quickly before one of us cries or decides to give one more hug.

Marilyn walks ahead of us and is walking briskly back to the van. She is in a hurry to get out of here and doesn't want to look back. I try to catch up with her, but her legs are so much longer than mine. Dana catches up with her, but she pushes him away when he tries to put his arm around her. We decide to give them their space. Maybe it is too hard for her because she doesn't have her family here either. Marilyn left her family behind in China and may never see them again.

We get in the van and are whisked away to the airstrip. Before we know it, we are boarding the plane home with just one stop in Halifax. The captain tells us we can stop any other place with immigration and customs but since Sam has a connection there it is easier. We agree and the plane takes off. None of us say very much during the flight.

We arrive in Oswego just as the sun is rising. We are all exhausted and want to get home as soon as possible. There are two cars waiting on the airstrip. One to take us back to town, the other to take Marilyn back to Home Base. But she tells the driver she's going with us. She wants to stay with Dana because he was so sick. I think she doesn't want to be alone. She seems very emotional.

The driver drops them off at Dana's apartment and then takes us home. There is no way I can go to class today. Marcos says he thinks he can make it, but by the time we are home he goes to sleep right away. Another day of missed classes. How are we going to keep our grades up if we continue like this?

I remember to text Mamá to let her know we are all back home safe. She returns an emoji with a heart and a snoopy. Sandy or Junior must have shown her how to use emojis. I send her a big heart in return. Then I fall into a deep sleep.

CHAPTER 17

The week is flying by, it's already Wednesday and we haven't been back to Home Base or to classes since last Thursday. Sam asks us to go to Home Base this morning for a mandatory meeting. Marcos and I hope it's not because we need to leave right away on another trip.

We both want to get a run in this morning before the meeting. We leave and decide to run across campus and down by the lake. It's been too long, and we feel the lack of exercise. I don't think our run will be a long one today. We circle back to campus and back home. Our driver will be at our apartment soon.

I check my phone and I see a text from Joy, '*Make sure you go to the mandatory meeting today.*'

I tell Marcos about the text, "Why would she think I won't show up? It's mandatory. We have to go. That's a strange text."

"Well, she is a bit over the top sometimes," Marcos says.

We get ready to go to the meeting and don't think too much about the text. The driver picks us up but isn't very talkative. He looks very serious. Maybe he's tired too. He stops to pick up Dana and Marilyn. We are all silent during the drive.

When we enter the driveway to Home Base, I look for Joy's car. I don't see it and think it's unusual. She is usually the first one here. Maybe her leg is bothering her, and she won't be here today.

Juan welcomes us into the house. He is sullen and walks us to Sam's office. Something is up and I don't think it is good news.

"Good morning everyone," Sam welcomes us all and tells us to take a seat. Mary Ellen is next to him. Now I know something is wrong because she hardly says anything and isn't smiling.

"Sam, by now we know something is wrong. Did something happen to one of the kids?" I ask.

"You are all well trained and observant. It's hard to hide our feelings when something is not right within our circle," he says.

"Oh no, that's why Joy sent that text. Is there something wrong with Joy?" I ask.

"Margarita, you never have let us tell you anything without jumping to conclusions. This time you are correct. Yes, there is an issue with Joy. But let me get to that in a minute," he says.

We all look at each other and wonder what can be happening with Joy.

"First of all, Dana, how are you feeling? It's hard when you are on a mission and your body gives out, isn't it? Don't feel bad about it, we are lucky it wasn't anything serious."

"I'm feeling much better. I have to admit when I was on the plane to Bear Island and got so sick there was nothing I could do. It was out of my control at that point. I'm so glad Marilyn was there with me," Dana says.

Mary Ellen speaks up and says, "This team is phenomenal. You always work well together and take care of each other. Our other teams aren't as close as this one."

"Absolutely, this mission was an excellent effort from everyone. I want to thank you all. You all stepped up when you needed to. This is an excellent team!"

Sam stares at Mary Ellen for a moment as if to ask her for guidance and support.

Dana speaks up and asks, "Is Joy alive?"

I have the same feeling that maybe something terrible has happened to Joy and I fear the worst. Since finding out about our WITSEC agents and their demise, I tend to jump to the worst case scenario when there is bad news.

"Yes, she is alive. She is well," Mary Ellen says.

Sam interrupts, "Joy will no longer be working with us."

"What? Why? What happened?" Marcos asks.

"She is our mentor and trained us. What happened, where is she?" I ask.

"Remember, Margarita, when you asked if you can ever quit? What was my answer?" He asks.

"You said, I could never leave but I could work in another agency or department associated with you," I say.

"Yes, exactly. Joy's injury is more serious than she first thought. She feels she'll be unable to lead anymore teams. Her leg is giving her lots of pain. She resigned yesterday."

"Wait, she can't resign. You said that," I say.

"No, she didn't resign from working for me, but resign from being here in Oswego and working from Home Base on rescue missions," he explains. "She will be working from another agency where there is less physically-demanding work. She doesn't feel she can keep up with the younger recruits. That was always her strength, her ability to lead and physically keep ahead of her trainees. She is no longer able to do that," he explains.

"What happens now? Do we stop going to the border to rescue kids? It's not over yet, there are more kids every day, aren't there?"

"Yes, more now than ever. We will continue with missions to the border. Mary Ellen and I have to make some big decisions. This was all too sudden. We should always have a Plan B in place, but this caught us off guard. We have a number of agents who could step into Joy's job, but none as well prepared as Joy. We have to do some thinking. For the mean time, we are going to stop recruiting. That is a great strength Joy has. We are going to stick to people we have already trained to complete the missions to the border," he says.

All four of us are silent. The news is a shock. Joy is our lifeline. We rely on her for any information when we can't contact Sam. We are going to miss her. We did resent her presence in our lives in the beginning because it felt like she was always popping up when we least expected her. Over time we grew to respect her. It will sad to work without her.

"When can we see her? Can we go to her house?" I ask.

"No, she's left town. Once her decision was made, we helped her leave town. It's part of our contract. She will take some time off and then start her next assignment," Mary Ellen explains.

"We can't see her? Can we text or call her?" I ask.

"No, she has asked that we don't give out her contact info. It's hard for her to leave this assignment, she loved it here," Sam says.

"Will we ever see her again?" Marilyn asks.

"There's a very small possibility your paths will cross over the next few years. But it's not probable."

"Margarita, Joy recommended you and but specifically wanted you to replace her in the transition. So, until further notice Margarita is lead for this group. Any questions?" He asks.

"Not from me," Dana says.

Marilyn smiles and says, "She is our leader already."

Marcos laughs and says, "I'm not surprised at all. No problem from me."

I am shocked but more shocked about Joy leaving. I am speechless. Marcos takes my hand and says, "You okay?"

"Yes, I'm just so shocked about Joy. She sent me a text last night and said to make sure I came to the meeting today. I thought it was a strange text, but I didn't know it was her last text. If I had known I would have texted her back. That number is probably disconnected now, right?"

"Yes, that number will be recycled, it's no longer in service," Mary Ellen says sadly.

"What about our trip to Bear Island this weekend? Are we still going with my family?" I ask.

"Oh, yes. We also got Yasmene and Miguel's NDA paperwork. That's one of the last things Joy turned in to us," Sam says.

"I think if you leave Friday night, you'll be able to attend classes on Friday. I assume you want to get back to your schoolwork as much as possible. We also need to talk some more about your studies, we have some ideas," Sam says as he holds up his hand, signaling he's not ready to discuss his final statement.

Dana and Marilyn look at each other and smile, "Sam can we go with them this weekend. We feel like part of their family too. We'd like to go with them. Is that okay?"

"If you want, we thought you'd like to rest. But, if you feel up to going, that's fine with us. The kids will be happy to see you," Mary Ellen says.

"Sure, go ahead. We don't have any of you lined up for a mission for a few weeks. Enjoy the weekend," Sam says.

We leave Home Base with new information. I'm not sure how I feel about any of it. I'm the leader of this group now. I hope I can do a great job. I don't want to disappoint anyone.

On the drive back to town we are all quiet. No one expected the news we got.

CHAPTER 18

Our classes seem to move on without us. We have a lot to catch up on, Professor Ricks tells us not to worry about his class. He knows where we have been. He says if we need to make up any grades, he will interview us individually and count it as an exam. The knowledge we are gaining is much more hands on that what he can provide in class. I try to point out that we aren't dealing with any forensics evidence, but he says this is a lower level class and not to worry. This summer he will go more in depth when we are all on Bear Island.

My language teacher and math teachers however aren't as forgiving. They both want to know how and when I'll catch up on the work I missed. I tell them I'll get the work to them as soon as possible. I missed two quizzes and a math lab. I'll have to figure out a way to get another math lab.

Marcos is just as busy with his classes. Every night we both stay up late to finish work. We don't hear from Marilyn or Dana the rest of the week either. I assume they are busy doing the same thing we are every night.

Sandy and Junior text me quite often and ask questions about Bear Island Camp. They are excited, but anxious. It sounds like they may be having second thoughts about moving away from their friends. I tell them it is so beautiful they will love it. They can always come back and stay with Marcos and I if they want to visit friends. We will be there all summer but will return in the fall for classes.

I ask about Ricardo and Memo and they tell me they are adjusting well. Papá has them helping in the kitchen. They need to close it down and prepare for the next owners. Every day they do inventory and clean. Since they aren't going to school here, they can help all day long. Mamá takes Memo to the library for story time and to meet other kids. Even though he won't be staying here in Oswego she thinks it's important to get him out with other kids his age. When Junior comes home, he invites both Ricardo and Memo to go play soccer with his friends from school. I worry they will like it here so much they won't want to return to Bear Island, but that's not a choice. The decision has been made.

Mamá calls us Thursday and asks us to come to dinner. I have to tell her no because we are so busy with homework. She asks if they can come over and drop off our dinner. I tell her that would be the greatest gift. We both need to focus on school before leaving for the weekend on Friday.

At six we hear a knock on the door and it's my whole family. I didn't expect everyone, I only expected my parents to drop off dinner. I realize maybe they need a break from Ricardo and Memo too. It has been a lot for them to take in two more kids.

Marcos invites everyone in, and I get the paper plates and silverware out. We have some soda in the fridge, and I grab that too. My parents have made a large tray of tacos, enchiladas and beans and rice. They tell us to eat as much as we want because they want to use up all of the fresh food before the weekend. Their last day at the taqueria is coming soon. It will be hard for them to walk away.

Ricardo and Memo seem to have fit in well with my family. When Memo whines about something Mamá says, "Memo use your words, what do you need? No whining, remember?"

I love that she is mothering him like she did with us. She isn't going to ignore he has been through a lot, but she also isn't going to put up with whining or crying.

Yasmene and Miguel are there with their kids. It is great to see everyone together. I'm so glad they signed their NDA. Now I can tell them most everything about Bear Island.

Because they know we are busy they don't stay long. Miguel helps Marcos clean up. The only ones missing are Dana and Marilyn.

We talk about what time to be ready for the car to pick them up. They are so excited to be able to be picked up like someone famous. I tell them it will be either two cars or one 15 passenger van. The pick-up for us is scheduled for 4 PM, I assume they will be picked up right after. Yasmene and Miguel say they will park their car out back of the taqueria. It will be one stop for them and another one to pick up Dana and Marilyn.

By 5 pm we should be able to take off. I remind them all to bring passports and ID. Hugs and kisses take us all a while and my last hug goes to Memo. He whispers in my ear, "Gracias Margarita. Are you my sister now?"

I give him an extra hug and whisper back, "Yes, I'm your sister."

When Marcos comes back in and closes the door, he looks at me and asks, "What? Why the sad face?"

"I'm not sad, I'm happy. Memo just asked me if I'm his sister and I said yes. I never thought when I left

San Felipe, I would end up with such a big family and so happy."

"We are a big family and a happy one. It's going to be great this weekend on Bear Island. I can't wait. But for now, I have more homework waiting. I need to turn in a full week's work tomorrow before we leave."

"Ok, me too. It was a nice dinner," I say.

We both go to our separate work areas and open our books. A lot is happening, and I need to finish my math.

Friday, Marcos and I rush to campus to class. We both have a packet of work to turn in to our professors. My math professor is surprised I got it done. My language professor wasn't surprised. Marcos and I both go to Professor Rick's class. Dana and Marilyn are there too. I can tell they are excited about the trip. We all try to pay attention to Professor Ricks, but I find myself thinking about the trip more than I should. This will be the first time we go to Bear Island and it's not an assignment. This time it's just to show my family around the island and introduce them to everyone.

I get texts all morning from Sandy. *'Are we still going for sure?'* My response is always the same: *'Yes!'*

It's a big deal for a teenager to relocate again. She's made a lot of friends here in Oswego. She's nervous.

I know once she's there she will love it. There are other teenagers there and Ricardo will introduce her to everyone. She'll now have an older brother to show her around.

After our last class we rush home to wait for our driver. I get one last call from my father and he asks, "Margarita, you are sure this is okay for us to fly to

Canada and return? They won't ask us to go through immigration?"

"Papá, what passport do you have? Is it Mexican or American? You have a United States passport now. It doesn't matter anymore," I say.

"Okay, hija. I just got nervous. Last minute jitters you know. I don't want any problems for my family."

"I understand, it takes a while to get used to. Since we are only going for the weekend, they will let us in on a tourist visa. When you move there, you'll receive a residential visa. It's all legal. I wouldn't put any of you in danger, you know that," I say.

"Yes, I know. ¡Gracias!"

"I'll see you later Papá. I can't wait to show you Bear Island," I say.

It's normal for him to worry after what we all have been through. It has only been a few years since I left San Felipe alone on my trip to live in Oregon. I thought they were all dead and they didn't know I was alive and traveling by Greyhound bus to Oregon.

We are all safe now. We just need to remember how lucky we are to be together.

The van pulls up in front of our apartment and Dana and Marilyn are already there. We rush out to the van with our bags and get in.

"This is so much fun, I can't wait. It's been a long week," I say.

"It sure has," Dana says.

"Let's go get everyone else. I know they are going to be so excited," Marcos says.

When we arrive behind the taqueria we see the luggage lined up. Each person has a bag so there are at least six bags, but I count ten. They weren't taught by Joy on how to pack a go bag. Sadness washes over me when I think of Joy, but it goes away quickly when I see Memo run out to the van.

"Hi. Are we really going to Bear Island? Do Ricardo and I have to stay?" Memo asks with a look of worry on his face.

"Yes, we are all going to Bear Island, but you get to come back when we do. When Mamá and Papá move there, you will go with them. Does that sound ok to you?"

"Sí, I want to stay with my family. Mamá says I can call her that. I want to stay with Mamá and Papá," Memo says.

This brings tears to my eyes but thankfully everyone comes to join us in the van. As soon as they are buckled in, we take off for the airstrip.

Everyone seems so excited. When we leave town, they start asking questions. They start to get nervous.

"Are we going to Rochester Airport?" Papá asks.

"How far until we get to the airport?" Junior asks.

Dana speaks up and answers them both, "We are almost there. We don't fly from Rochester; we are going to an airstrip outside of town. Ricardo and Memo know because they landed there a few days ago."

When we drive up to the plane Sam and Mary Ellen are waiting for us. I'm surprised to see them there, but then realize they haven't met Yasmene and Miguel and their family.

Sam steps forward and reaches his hand out to them, "Hello, nice to meet you finally. This is Mary Ellen my assistant."

"Nice to meet you too," answer both Yasmene and Miguel.

"Mary Ellen brought your temporary badges; we'll need to update them when you get back. But she would like to draw some blood for your files. She has the necessary medical supplies on the plane. Do you mind?"

"Is it necessary right now? They can't wait until we get back?" I ask.

"Margarita, if it weren't necessary Mary Ellen wouldn't do it. She needs to have their medical info on file for insurance purposes. Today is their first day of being part of the team. We want them to have all the benefits you have. Yes, it's necessary."

"Okay, it's alright Margarita," Yasmene says and steps forward.

My parents already had been to Home Base and had their IDs and blood tests done. Ricardo and Memo ask if they need any tests. The reply is no because they are part of Bear Island Camp. We wait outside for Mary Ellen to finish. When Mary Ellen comes down the portable stairway and says she has what she needs we all say goodbye to her and also to Sam.

The kids run up the stairs to be the first on the plane.

The kids sit together, and Ricardo and Memo tell the others they can watch cartoons on the portable players. They both rush up front to grab one for each kid. The headphones are in the pockets. It is nice to see they are all happy.

Mamá and Papá decide to sit near the kids. Everyone else sits behind them. We aren't working and this is a short vacation for us. The attendants come through the cabin and welcome us aboard. They tell us we'll be landing in Halifax in about three hours and we should sit back and relax. Dinner will be served after take-off.

My parents smile because they are used to being the ones serving the food. It's a luxury to be served.

The flight is uneventful and soon we are on final approach to Halifax I tell everyone to please have their IDs and passports ready. Immigration will come aboard and ask to see them.

This time the agents come aboard and are surprised to see each person hand them their passports. They are used to me or Joy handling everything. They tell me next time it's easier if I give them all of the passports. I let them know on the return trip we will do it that way. They thank us and leave.

"Did I hear them say we are going to Canada?" Sandy asks.

"Yes, didn't I tell you? Bear Island is in Canada. Off the coast of Nova Scotia."

"Maybe, I guess I didn't pay attention," she answers. "I was so excited I didn't listen."

"You'll like it, it's beautiful there," Ricardo tells her. I can tell he likes to be a big brother.

We take off and are soon airborne again. Dana leans over and says, "Glad we didn't make a stop at the hospital this time."

"So are we!" Marcos and I say together.

I can tell my family is very excited, not just because of the trip, because we are all here together. And now we have Ricardo and Memo too.

Everyone is so relaxed, and the kids are getting along so well. I squeeze Marco's hand and tell him to look at Sandy, Ricardo, Junior and Memo. "Don't they look so happy?" I ask.

"Yes, and we helped Ricardo and Memo get here. I'm so glad Sam found us and asked us to help out," Marcos says.

"For sure. I wouldn't have it any other way, except to not have them ever separated from their parents. That would be even better, but they got separated, I'm glad we could help," I say.

The flight seems so short this time and soon we are approaching Bear Island. Everyone is trying to get a window seat so they can watch. It's already dark so they can only see the lights on the island.

Once again Memo asks me if he and Ricardo can return with the family when we leave. I assure him he can. He smiles and returns to his seat. My parents turn around and smile. They are just as excited as the kids.

Once we land, we can see two vans approach the plane on the airstrip. There are no fifteen passenger vans here, so we'll have to split up. Marcos and I decide to split the kids up and have them go with us and leave the adults to go in the other van. Everyone is so excited they don't care. Marilyn and Dana go with my parents.

Soon we are driving away from the plane and approaching the parking lot near the lodge.

"There are so many Christmas trees," Junior says.

"It smells like Christmas," Sandy laughs. Marco smiles when he hears this.

There is a group waiting at the edge of the path to welcome us. They all wave at us. I see Adriana and Rosa with their mentor. I'm sure they are eager to see Ricardo and Memo.

When we exit the vans our welcoming crew rushes forward to give us hugs and shake hands with my parents. They ask my parents if they want to ride in the golf cart, but they say no, they will walk with everyone else.

Ricardo leads the group. Memo takes my mother and father by the hands. He says, "We'll show you around."

It surprises me because when he left Bear Island he was still in his state of silence. I guess he was observing more than we thought.

Ricardo leads us inside the Lodge and tells everyone, "This is where we eat our meals. We also help in the kitchen. Mamá says, "This is wonderful. They help clear and clean the dishes every meal?"

"Yes, and they take turns," I say.

"Is this where we will be working?" Papá asks.

"Yes, I think so. I think you'll manage all of the food on the island. The cook will explain what you need to do," I say.

Yasmene and Miguel ask where they will be working. I explain that after dinner we'll take a tour and we'll show them the school and the medical center. Later on, they'll see where they will live.

I'm not sure where Marcos and I will stay tonight. I wonder if the cabin where we normally stay is where they'll put my family. We are used to the little cabin they give us. Maybe it is too small for the others.

"This place is fun. You should see their kitchen Papá. It is huge. They have a huge walk-in cooler and freezer," Junior says.

"You can show me later, hijo." Papá says.

Memo speaks up and says, "I can show you where I used to sleep. I lived in the medical center with Ricardo. Will we live in a cabin now with you?" He asks.

"Yes, I think so," Papá answers.

Mama and Papa want to see the kitchen. They follow Adriana into the kitchen.

"Oh my. This is a wonderful kitchen. I think I'll like cooking here," Mamá says.

Adriana shows her around and introduces her to the kitchen staff. Papá joins them and I can tell by the smile on his face he likes it here too.

Ricardo says, "I am so glad they are moving here to Bear Island. I'm also grateful we can stay with them."

"Ricardo, they are very happy to have you and Memo as part of the family. Let's go for our tour. I think everyone will want to see where they will sleep tonight."

When we leave the kitchen, I see Dana speaking with one of the mentors. They have the sleeping arrangements. Dana comes toward the group with the list in his hand.

"Margarita and Marcos, you are in the same cabin you usually stay. Marilyn and I are next door. Your parents are in the next group of housing. We'll need to take two of the golf carts to show them where it is, it's a little bit farther away," Dana explains.

"Okay, let's do that. We can get them settled. It is getting late, they may just want to rest," I say.

My parents crowd around us and ask what we are doing next. We explain their cabin is a ways away and we need to take golf carts.

"That sounds like fun, let's go. We want to see where we will live," Mamá says.

I was worried they may want to be right next to us, but it doesn't seem like it matters at all. They seem happy with everything.

We load into the golf carts with their luggage and take them to their cabin. Yasmene and Miguel and their children follow along in a third golf cart because their house is near my parents. I can tell they are interested to see where they will live also. They have been living in a small apartment and I know space is tight. I can't wait to show them their cabin.

When we drive over a small hill, we can see a circle of cabins in the distance, all with lights on and it gives the idea of a Christmas card. The houses are against a backdrop of tall fir trees and there is a stone path that leads up to the doorway of each house. Between the hill and the houses is a big picnic area and playground. There are picnic tables, fire pits for barbecue and swings and playground equipment.

My mamá's eyes grow bigger and bigger as we get closer to the cabin. Their cabin has a front porch with a swing, and on the other side a table with six chairs. On the table is a red-checked tablecloth and a pitcher filled with daisies. It is beautiful. I'm not sure who puts together the welcoming cabins, but they do a great job.

We pull up in front of the cabin and Sandy and Junior jump out and run up the steps.

"Is this our house?" Sandy asks.

"Yes, it will be when you move here," I say.

"I can't wait," Junior says.

Everyone follows them inside to see a huge living room with a gigantic stone fireplace. Someone has left the fireplace lit and it gives such welcoming atmosphere. On the opposite wall from the fireplace is a log staircase. The kids all run upstairs and find four bedrooms. We can hear them each claiming a room. Ricardo and Memo say they want to be in the same room. There is a large master suite for my parents.

"This is unbelievable," Mamá says. "Are you sure this is for us?"

"Yes, it is part of your benefits. Your housing is included. Since you have such a big family now you get one of the biggest cabins. It's okay."

I can see Yasmene and Miguel are smiling and getting anxious. I know they want to see if their cabin is as nice as Mamá's.

Across the big circle of houses is a cabin almost as big, but only one floor. It still looks beautiful. There is a big porch on the front, but it also wraps around the whole cabin to the back. The lights are on and we rush over to see Yasmene and Miguel's house. We let them go in first, but we are not far behind. When we enter, we see a grand room with a cathedral ceiling made of knotty pine. The kitchen is off to the side but is open to the family room. There is a big fireplace on the left and the fire is roaring. I can tell this is going to be a great place for them.

At the end of the hall is the master suite with a bathroom. The two other bedrooms have a bathroom in between.

"This is so beautiful, there is so much room. I can't believe we get to live here," Yasmene says.

"It's true, you get to live here. Look, there's a door at the end of the hallway in this direction. Let's see what is there.

When we open the door, we are amazed to see a porch. We go out on the porch and there is a swing to sit on for two people and then chairs for others. Yasmene and Miguel sit down on the swing and start to glide back and forth. Their kids wander around the porch and then return to sit with them.

"This is so beautiful. I can't even explain how I feel right now," Miguel says.

"Where do you stay, Margarita and Marcos? Is your house nearby?" Sandy asks.

"Ours is a cabin back closer to the lodge. We only stay overnight once in a while, but now that you are all here, we may spend more time here," I say.

"Why don't we all rest up and get settled. We can meet up again for breakfast. If you want to wander around or go for a walk you are welcome to go wherever you want. Just make sure you take someone with you. We don't want anyone to get lost. We can check out the school tomorrow," Marcos says.

Yasmene says. "I'd like to look around the house, it is so beautiful."

Each family group goes back to their own area. I watch as Ricardo and Memo follow my parents and I feel the tears coming. Marcos looks at me and says, "Time for us to take a break. You need some more rest."

"I'm so happy it worked out for them. I worry what will happen if their dad or Abuelita are found."

"Don't worry right now. Let's go and get some sleep. We both need it," he says as he grabs my hand and starts walking back to our cabin.

Bear Island Camp

CHAPTER 19

The next morning, we hear a knock on the door, and we open it to find Ricardo and Memo standing on the doorstep. We must have slept in.

Memo blurts out, "Mamá and Papá are waiting for you. They want to take a tour and find the school." Ricardo blushes to hear Memo call my parents Mamá and Papá. I smile and pat him on the shoulder.

"I'm sure they'd love it if you called them that too," I say.

"It's hard for me. My mamá died and I don't know where my Papá is. It seems a little disrespectful to them if I call them Mamá and Papá."

"Maybe you can call them something else then. You come up with a name that feels comfortable to you. How about that?" I say.

"Ok, that sounds better. I'll think about it," he says.

We close the door and follow them down to the space in front of the lodge. Everyone is there waiting except for us. We all go into the lodge to grab a breakfast.

When we leave the lodge there are enough golf carts for all of us to go on the tour. We have the head mentor there to help us. We haven't even seen the entire island yet. He leads the way with Marilyn and Dana. Sandy and Junior ride along with them.

Next are Yasmene and Miguel. In the next cart are Mamá and Papá, Ricardo and Memo. Marcos and I follow up the parade. It is quite a procession. The day is sunny and warm and a great day for a field trip.

First, we drive past the medical center where we all visited last night. The mentor tells us there is a doctor and nurse on staff twenty-four hours a day. They live in a cabin near the medical center. For serious issues they can contact a MediVac helicopter to fly the patient to the Halifax hospital. We are closer to medical care here than in many places. No one should have to worry about getting in to see a doctor. The best thing he says, "It's all included. If you are a resident of Bear Island your medical care is taken care of. That is huge benefit."

Dana shouts back, "Yes in case you end up in a hospital in Halifax. You don't have to worry about the bill. I know, I was there last week."

"We are so glad you aren't there now, Dana," Marcos yells back.

We all clap and cheer to the fact that Dana is with us and not in the hospital.

"Next, we are going to go past the playground. I think you probably saw that on your way to your cabins. During the day, the children are allowed on the playground if there is one mentor present. Later on, those rules may loosen up when everyone gets to know the place. Soon people like Ricardo and Adriana will be able to supervise the younger ones once we are all on a school schedule."

I see Ricardo's face redden with embarrassment, "He says Sandy too, right?"

"Of course, once she is settled in like everyone else," he says with a smile.

We continue past the playground and basketball courts, past the first circle of cabins and over the hill. As we pass the circle of houses where my family will live, I hear them cheer and point to their house. They all appear to be very happy.

The pathway curves around to the right and comes to a stop sign. Here there is a sign that points to the lodge if you go right. On top of that sign are other signs. One says in bright red letters BEACH, the next one is bright green letters SCHOOL, the other one in orange letters says CHAPEL and the last sign says MAINTENANCE.

We all take a left and follow the first golf cart. He slows as we come to the chapel. He pulls up to a stop and asks us to turn off our golf carts.

"Here is a chapel, anyone who wants to worship here can. There isn't an organized group here on the island, but everyone does their own thing. Sometimes on Sunday nights there is a worship group here. I haven't been yet, so I don't know anything about it. You are all welcome to sign up for a worship time if you have a group. Sometimes some of the young people come here and work on activities. Okay, let's move on now to the school," he says.

We all are excited to see the school. Up to five-hundred kids or more will be living here and need a school. We drive across a field; there isn't a building yet, but it is under construction. As we pull up, I see Miguel is very excited. This is where he will teach this summer.

"This is the school building that is set to be completed in a month's time," he says.

We all look at each other with surprise. It doesn't even have the walls started. All we can see is the foundation. Near the construction site we see some containers like you see on a train. There are ten containers. One is marked furniture, the other windows, the other wiring, the other plumbing, supplies and other unlabeled items.

"You might think it's unbelievable, but in a month this school will be ready to have the interior outfitted. It may be longer than a month before students will be in their classes but definitely before summer," he says.

Dana speaks up, "Well if Sam has any say about it, it will be finished for sure. He makes sure everything gets done."

"Yes, that's true. Your houses you just moved into weren't finished a month ago. They were on the schedule for summer, but he called and said they needed to be done asap. So, they were finished asap," he says with a smile.

"Is this where I'll be working this summer?" Miguel asks.

"Yes, by the time you are here it will be finished. In the meantime, I can show you where the students are meeting now."

We all jump back into our golf carts and follow him back to the path. He once again turns left, and we follow him a little bit farther. We see a big building that looks like it could be a grocery store or warehouse. On the front is a sign that says, Community Center Store. We look at the building and I decide it has to be huge inside. It looks like a gymnasium from a high school or from campus. It's tall, wide and long.

"Okay, let's take a tour. I'll show you around and tell you what this place is designed to be. It is labeled community center, but it is a lot more than that, follow me," he says.

Inside the community center is a store with basics. There are a few groceries, but he informs us that when you live here you can do a weekly order and they bring what you want. Most people get their basic groceries in the once-a-week-box but come to the store for things they may run out of like milk, eggs or ice cream. The shelves hold a few items, but it isn't anything like a regular grocery store. Since we get our meals at the lodge, we don't need to buy groceries. But others may decide they want to eat at home.

Also, in the store are t-shirts, sweatshirts and winter coats. Along one wall are snow boots. Sandy and Junior look at us as Junior asks, "Will it snow a lot here?"

Marcos and I don't know so we ask the mentor.

"It can snow, but mostly the boots are to keep your feet warm. It gets very cold here and your normal tennis shoes won't keep your feet warm. You all will need a pair of warm boots.

"We have boots, hats and gloves because we live in Oswego, but it's nice to know we can get them here if we need to," Papá says.

We walk outside of the store and enter another door to a long hallway. It looks like a school but also looks like it could be an office building. Our mentor takes us first to the front office. He shows Miguel where to find things and introduces him to the office staff and head teacher.

"This is Miguel, he will be doing his student teaching here this summer. I'm giving him a tour of the school."

"There is a class in the gym if you want to go in and watch. I don't think the teacher will mind," one of the receptionists says.

"How many teachers work here?" Miguel asks.

"Right now, four teachers and four assistants. The assistants alternate between office duties and helping in the classroom. Usually they are wives or husbands of the teachers. We try to recruit teachers whose spouse would be willing to come here and live and work. It is usually easy to find couples who are interested."

"How about when the new school opens? Will you need more teachers?" Miguel asks.

"It depends on how many more kids Sam decides to bring here. The school is built for five hundred students. Much more than that and it will be hard to keep up with housing needs. A lot of the kids live with mentors in a bunkhouse. If we don't find their parents, we try to move them to a more permanent situation with a family. That is a process we haven't figured out yet," he says.

Dana and Marilyn look at Marcos and I; we know what that means. That means there are four hundred more kids in detention centers waiting to be rescued. This makes us uneasy; we are tired but don't want those kids waiting to be rescued. I hope Sam has another team who can help bring those kids here.

In the gym the kids are playing volleyball. There is a net set up in the middle of the gym. The kids stop and look when we enter the gym. They recognize us and start to wave and run toward us. We tell them to go back to their game. We can check in on them later.

Dana and Marcos ask the teacher if they can join. The teacher welcomes them over. Memo, Ricardo, Marilyn, Miguel, Sandy and Junior also join in to even out the teams. What a great place! Most of the kids seem healthy and happy. It warms my heart to see them smiling and laughing.

The teacher blows the whistle and tells the kids to gather around him. They already know us, but introduces Mamá, Papá, Sandy, Junior, Miguel and Yasmene. He tells them Mamá and Papá will be working in the kitchen, Yasmene will be in the medical center, and Miguel will be here as a teacher.

Miguel says hello to them and then tells them he speaks Spanish and is excited to come to work at the school. They start to ask if he can stay, he explains he needs to go back and finish his classes but will be back this summer. They all cheer to hear he will be working with them over the summer. The teacher sends them on to their next class. We watch as they leave the gym and grab their backpacks from a hook outside the door.

Miguel says, "What an opportunity to work with such nice kids! I can't believe it. I was a little worried about teaching in a high school in Oswego where class sizes are almost thirty-five to a classroom. This sounds more like fun."

We agree this is a great opportunity. Sandy and Junior want to know if they can go see a class they will be in. The mentor says since it is between classes we can go see if the teacher will allow it. We follow him down the hall.

The classes are divided by levels, not necessarily by grade or age. The literacy levels and English skills help to put students where they need to be. The math classes are also divided by level. There are two teachers for middle and high school. The other two teachers are for elementary students. The division is about equal now, but each time a new group comes in they never know the ages of the kid coming in.

Sandy and Junior will both be in the middle school and high school group. They have combined classes until the new school opens. As soon as we walk up to the door Adriana jumps up and grabs Junior and Sandy's hand to welcome them into the classroom. Ricardo joins them too.

The mentor says he needs to check with the teacher, but the teacher waves and says it's okay. Adriana already told the class because she met us last night when we arrived. Sandy and Junior would be joining the class. They both look very excited as they join the class of ten other students.

Memo will start classes with Rosa when he returns in the summer. He had still been under medical care before we took him with us to Oswego. He is eager to see his class, so we walk down the hall to Rosa's class. She waves when she sees him. He turns and asks if he can stay in the class.

"We need to ask the teacher permission Memo," Mamá says.

The mentor goes to speak with the teacher, and she gives her okay. Memo runs over to sit next to Rosa. He is so excited to be with her. He hasn't experienced very many things here on Bear Island.

Miguel asks if he can stay with Memo in his class. He explains to the teacher he will be working as a student teacher this summer and he would like to observe if possible. She waves him in also.

The rest of us exit the school. There is no reason to worry about the kids, they can all find their way back and Memo is with Miguel.

We go down to another entrance on the side of the building.

"Francesca and Luis, you'll be interested in what's inside here. All of the food is stored here for the whole island. For the construction workers, the kids and staff," the mentor says.

"Wow, this is huge," Papá says as he eyes the tall shelves that line the room.

Along each wall there are tall metal shelves with cases of canned foods, sacks of flour and sugar. One area has twenty-pound bags of pinto beans and rice. Another area is stacks of cases of fruit juices, snacks, crackers, and peanut butter. On the far wall there are two large metallic doors. One is for the deep freeze. When they open the door, we see a deep freezer with shelves of meat, chicken, and other frozen foods. I see on one of the shelves a large box of frozen fish. CongaPesca is the name on the box. I point this out to Marcos, and he smiles. The same company we started working at in Fish Camp. What a coincidence that the same company is where we buy our fish. It gives me a minute to think about the days we were on the ship and hardly knew each other. It seems so long ago, so much has happened since Fish Camp. We escaped the Sea Breeze, met up with my family who we thought had been killed in an accident. We were then put into WISTEC for our protection from Tío Enrique and his associates.

I start to feel dizzy and I need to sit down. It doesn't feel like a panic attack but I'm dizzy. I feel like if I don't sit down, I'll fall down. Marcos grabs my hand and walks me out of the freezer to find a place to sit. No one else notices until they also exit the freezer.

They start to walk over to the large fridge, but Mamá sees me sitting down and rushes over.

"What's wrong hija? Are you sick?" She asks.

"No, I just got a little dizzy, that's all. I'm fine," I say as I stand up.

The tour of the refrigerator is short because now they are concerned about me.

"This is where all of the orders you make will arrive. Since you two will be in charge of food services you will be doing the ordering and inventory here," The mentor says.

"This is a huge responsibility," my Papá says.

"You will have lots of help and training, don't worry," the mentor answers.

We start to walk out, and Marcos says, "I'm going to take Margarita back to rest. You can all go ahead and finish the tour."

"Are you sure?" Papá asks.

"Yes, we'll get her a cold drink and rest. We've been doing a lot of flying and I think she is exhausted," Marcos says.

Marcos drives me back to our cabin in the golf cart. By the time we reach the front door I know I'm going to be sick. I rush to the bathroom and make it just in time. Marcos follows me.

"I knew you weren't okay, but I didn't know you had an upset stomach," Marcos says with concern.

"I didn't either until I walked into that deep freeze, brought back so many memories," I say.

"Let's get you on the sofa, or do you want to go to bed?" He asks.

"No, the sofa is fine. I know Mamá will stop by. It'll be easier if I'm out here in the family room," I say.

"Okay, I'll get you some tea. Be right back," Marcos says as he tucks me in.

I don't get to drink the tea until it's cold. I wake up and realize I've been sound asleep for over an hour. Mamá is sitting at the kitchen table with Marcos. I hear them talking in whispers, but I can't tell what they are talking about.

I sit up and feel much better. I decide to join them in the kitchen. I surprise them as I hear the word doctor mentioned.

"I'm feeling much better now. It must have been something I ate or all of the flights. Who knows? But I do feel better now," I say

Marcos stands up to get me a fresh cup of tea. "Your Mamá thinks you should go over to the medical center."

"Why? I'm just overtired. You know that," I say.

"Hija, you've been so busy taking care of other people. Now is the time to take care of yourself. Please go see the doctor. It might be exhaustion or the flu. Or maybe…?"

"What?" I ask.

"Well, is there a possibility you might be pregnant?" She asks.

"No, I don't think…" I stammer.

"Maybe?" She asks.

"I've been so busy," I say.

"It's a possibility. Babies don't wait until you aren't busy. It's usually when babies like to make an appearance. Just when you least expect it. Maybe you aren't, but why not check with the doctor here to be sure," she says.

"Mamá, I need to finish school and I want to join the FBI. Marcos and I have plans. This wasn't part of our plans," I say.

I think of the other four-hundred kids waiting to be rescued, how can this be? I need to go help them. Sam has us on the schedule for summer school. Maybe I should go just to prove I'm not pregnant.

"I'm going to walk over to the medical center with Mamá. She wants me to get checked out. I'm sure it's nothing."

"I'll go with you," Marcos says.

"No, you don't need to. Take a break and get some fresh air. We won't be long. Mamá wants to go with me, okay?" I say.

"I guess, but you'll tell me right away what the doctor says?" He asks.

"Of course, we won't be long. It's just down the path. Things are so convenient here you know," I smile.

"Maybe I'll find Ricardo and see if he wants to shoot some hoops. I'll be down on the basketball court," Marcos says as he kisses me on the cheek.

Mamá and I walk to the medical center. I'm not sure what I hope will happen. We do want to have children, we just didn't plan on it so soon. I want to finish my studies and who knows if we would continue working with Sam or try to get into the FBI. He did say we couldn't leave so maybe the FBI is no longer an option. I guess what we are doing might be better. A baby? Really? I don't know if I can handle it. I wonder how Marcos will respond.

"Hija, don't worry until you find out the test results, okay? I can see you already are worrying. I see it on your face," Mamá says as she grabs my hand.

"You're right. I need to find out first. No need to worry until we know," I say.

We walk up the steps to the medical center and open the door. When we walk in the nurse is sitting up front and working on paperwork.

"Hi Margarita, how can I help you and your mother?" She asks.

"I need to see a doctor. Is anyone available?" I ask.

"Sure, let me go see who has time to see you," she says.

When she returns, she tells me to follow her to one of the examination rooms. The doctor enters and greets us. I tell the doctor I need a pregnancy test he tries to not look surprised, but his face betrays him.

"When was your last period?"

"I think a month or six weeks ago. I've been traveling a lot, I'm not sure."

"Okay, let's first do a urine test then we'll draw some blood to check your labs in case it's negative. Are you comfortable with that?" He asks.

"Yes, can you determine if I'm pregnant with those tests?" I ask.

"We can try. How long have you been feeling tired?" He asks.

"Well, the last two weeks have been very hectic. We flew a lot, had classes and came here twice. I thought it was from work," I say.

"Could be, but the flying can also mess up your cycle, but let's run those tests. I'm also going to run a test for anemia," he says.

"Okay, let's do it. I need to know," I say.

"Okay, we'll get the results in a few minutes," he says.

"Yes, we'll wait," I answer

While we are waiting, Marcos arrives. The nurse sends him back to us. He looks worried and rushes to find out what the doctor said.

"What did the doctor say? Did he say it's exhaustion? Does he want you to take some time off?" He asks.

"He will tell us soon. We are waiting for the results. He checked for anemia," I say. "We just need to wait. Sit down Marcos you are making me nervous."

"He also ran a pregnancy test. It might be too early but Mamá asked me to get a test to see if I'm pregnant. She thinks some of my symptoms are from pregnancy."

Marco's face turns from worry to a smile, "Well, it is a thought."

I look at Marcos and smile, "Yes, it is a thought, I just wasn't thinking we were ready for this."

"It will be okay. I'm glad we came in to see the doctor."

The doctor returns with a print-out in his hand, "Well, we have two positives. You are anemic and you are also pregnant. We need to get you started on some prenatal vitamins asap."

I'm in shock, it wasn't in my plan. What will I do now? How can I work for Sam? My whole family is coming here to live, and I will be a mother.

I see Marcos smile and he reaches over to pull me into a hug. Mamá is so happy she can't stop smiling. They both look at me and say, "Margarita, are you okay?"

The next thing I know I am in a bed in the medical center. My eyes barely open before I hear Marcos ask me, "Are you okay? What happened?"

The nurse checks my blood pressure and asks Marcos to step back and give me some room. "I think the news may have been a shock," Mamá says.

The doctor comes back in and says, "Her blood pressure dropped. I think she is extremely exhausted along with anemic. She needs bed rest. I'd like to keep her here overnight. She can rest at home tomorrow.

"But doctor, I can rest in my cabin. I'd like to go home," I plead.

"No, you are exhausted and need total bedrest for 24 hours. No arguments," he answers.

"The doctor is right. You need to rest. If you stay here, you won't be tempted to jump up and do things. You rest and Marcos or I will be here with you," Mamá says.

"No, actually I want no visitors for her until dinner time. One of you can come back to eat dinner with her. Other than that, no visitors!" The doctor says vehemently.

Marcos leans over to give me a kiss and says, "I'll be back for dinner. You sleep as much as you want. I need you to get better. Don't worry about a thing."

"I'll be fine. You go and spend time with everyone. Tell them I'm fine," I say.

Mamá kisses me on the cheek and leaves with Marcos. I know they both want to stay with me, but I am still drowsy and feel a little relief I don't have to think about anything except sleep.

The nurse comes in and checks my blood pressure a couple of times, but other than that I have no one with me. The nurse asks if I need anything and I assure her I just want quiet and rest. She leaves me and I drift off to sleep once again.

I hear Marcos talking to the nurse outside my room. He asks if I have rested and if the doctor has been in to see me.

"No, the doctor won't need to see her unless something new happens. He just wants her to rest. Her dinner will be here soon, did you bring dinner for yourself?"

"No, I wanted to make sure she was able to have visitors," I hear him say.

"I'll tell them to bring two trays and you can eat dinner together," the nurse says and smiles.

"Thanks, is it okay if I go in?" I hear him ask.

"Go ahead."

I see him walk into the room and feel a little better just at the sight of him. I rested all day and feel much better. Maybe the doctor will let me go home tonight.

"Hey, how are you feeling?" Marcos asks.

"A lot better. I slept all day. I only woke up when the nurse came in to check on me. How was your day?" I ask.

"Not bad, everyone is worried about you, but we took the kids down to the playground and they played and Dana, Ricardo and I played basketball. It's a wonderful place here," he says.

"I hope we get to live here. Since I'm pregnant, how am I going to work for Sam? He may not want us here if both of us can't work missions," I say.

"Don't worry, Sam knows you are here for a rest. He sends wishes for total recovery. He knows we've been working and going to school non-stop. He's worried he may have caused you stress by putting you in Joy's job. He says we'll talk when you feel better."

"And everyone else? Did you and Mamá tell them I'm pregnant?" I ask.

"No, Mamá and I decided you need to be there when we tell everyone, it's not news for us to share until you are ready."

The dinner trays arrive, and I realize I am very hungry. I see they have included lots of milk, cottage cheese, vegetables and a steak. They sure want me to get stronger!

Marcos says, "I'm glad I'm eating dinner with you. I think there was spaghetti for dinner in the lodge tonight. I love spaghetti but this steak is delicious!"

"I agree, it tastes so good!" I say between bites of steak.

Marcos smiles at me and asks, "Has it sunk in yet that we are going to have a baby? I'm so excited."

"Well, it was a shock but I'm getting use to the idea especially if I get to eat dinner like this every night. I worry about not being able to work on missions and bring more kids, but that could be temporary. We will have to wait to see what Sam says. I remember when Mary Ellen first gave me my physical, she asked if I could be pregnant. I asked if I was pregnant if Sam would withdraw the job offer," I say.

"What did she answer?" Marcos asks.

"She said no, but it would mean different training and different job assignments. Maybe they will move me to a different job," I say.

"Are you okay with that?" Marcos asks.

"Well, I have to be. I don't think I can do all of the flying that's required to get four hundred more kids to Bear Island. I don't want to even think about those kids waiting to be rescued. It makes me want to get out of this bed and go pick up some more kids," I say.

"No, that's not going to happen. Not until the doctor says you can. Even then we need to make sure you are strong enough. Let's take it slow, okay?" Marcos says.

"You know I don't want to take it slow when it comes to rescuing those kids. But you are right I don't have the strength right now to physically get on a plane and fly to the border."

"I'm glad to hear you say that. I know you can be stubborn and was worried you wouldn't listen to the doctor," Marcos admits.

"Let's finish dinner and I want to walk around a little. I don't think I need to be in bed without walking around."

The nurse walks in and hears my comment about taking a walk. "Yes, the doctor wants you to go take a short walk and get some fresh air, but not too far."

"Don't worry, we won't go far," I say.

Marcos and I walk out the front doors of the medical center and the fresh air hits me in the face. I needed to get that Bear Island fresh air. The smell of pine needles and the salty breeze coming off the bay is just what I need.

"This feels so good. I need rest but I also need to be outside. I know that the air here is good for me. I wish we could come to live here sooner. My family will be here, and we'll be back in Oswego. It will be hard at first," I say.

"Let's get you strong again. Stop worrying," Marcos says as he turns me around to walk back to the medical center.

The next morning the doctor says I can go back to my cabin if I promise to rest and not exert myself. Marcos meets me at the front door of the medical center and smiles when he sees doctor has released me.

When we arrive at the cabin, Marcos wants me to rest. I tell him I want to go to see my parents and show them I am fine. He agrees if I say I'll go in the golf cart and not walk.

"Walking is the best thing for me. I need exercise," I whine.

"Well, give yourself a day at least. Let me baby you a little," he says.

"Okay, but don't go overboard, I'm fine," I say.

When we pull up to my parents cabin, everyone is sitting on the front porch. Papá is wearing a new t-shirt with Papa Bear written on the front. He holds up another shirt for my mother with Mama Bear on the front. We all laugh when we see her put it on over her other shirt.

As soon as I see Ricardo I say, "You now have a new name to call them. Papa and Mama Bear. It looks like they have their Bear Island names. You think you can call them that?" I ask.

He smiles and says, "Yes, those are perfect names for them."

Marcos whispers in my ear, "Maybe we can get one made with Baby Bear on it."

I smile and say, "Let's wait until we tell them."

CHAPTER 20

My parents moved in April and have been working there ever since. Mama and Papa Bear are loved by everyone. They do all of the food ordering for the whole island, they supervise the warehouse, store and the kitchen at the lodge. Every night they are in the lodge cooking dinner. They feel like it is home and are so happy to live there.

Yasmene and Miguel both returned to their jobs and studies. But they were also excited to move up their schedule. Miguel was able to get his student teaching set for Spring and Yasmene also got her practicum moved up. They moved to Bear Island in May.

Marilyn, Dana, Marcos and I go back to our classes. We study hard and have to only fit in one mission before the end of the school year. Once again it was successful, and we were able to bring fifty more kids to Bear Island. The doctor asked me to stop flying as much. I could help with missions, but he only wanted me to fly to Bear Island and stay put for the summer. The baby is due in January and the flights to Bear Island are short enough, but the long-distance flights of rehoming kids and picking up the next group can be exhausting. I decided to finish the last mission and then listen to the doctor.

Sam developed a program with the professors at SUNY Oswego to be able to do online studies for the remainder of our program. We can graduate with our degrees in Forensics by completing the classes from our cabin on Bear Island. Dana and Marilyn can decide to stay in Oswego or join us on Bear Island. I think I know what decision they will make since they are planning a Fall wedding on Bear Island.

When we got the news of the baby, Marcos and I were very excited. We talked about what our plans had been before we found we were going to be parents. The dream of doing investigations for the FBI was always a goal. Now that goal seems to have shifted. If we have a family of our own, we need to change our plans. When we signed up to work for Sam, he told us we could never leave, but could work in different jobs or agencies. We decided to talk to Sam about what we wanted to do.

Our proposal was to work remotely from Bear Island in whatever capacity he could offer us. He was excited to hear about our baby, but a bit dismayed to hear I'd have to cut back on missions.

"You know Margarita, we never expect our agents to stay forever. They often move on to other positions or agencies. But Mary Ellen and I were hoping to keep your team together. You, Marcos, Marilyn and Dana are a great team. Let me think about what we can do. Give me a couple of days, okay?"

"Whatever you can do Sam is fine with us. We are so appreciative of everything you have done for us," I say.

Marcos adds, "We can still run a 3-person team for missions. Margarita will be missed but I'm sure Dana and Marilyn would like to continue."

"Okay, let me think. I'll get back to you soon," Sam says.

We never expected the news that Sam came up with. It was a huge surprise. Sam called us all to Home Base for a meeting.

"This feels like the old days, doesn't it?" Dana says.

"Yes, it does. Before I knew Sam, I could have never imagined all of the things we've done," Marcos says.

Marilyn smiles and says, "And you have no idea what he'll ask us to do in the future!"

Our meeting with Sam was in his office as always. We sit down and wait for him to give us his ideas.

"You guys ready for your next step?" Sam asks.

"Yes," we answer in unison.

"First, let me tell you what a great team this has been. You all stepped up and made the rescue of those kids a success."

We look at each other and smile. What will he say next I wonder?

"Mary Ellen and I want to keep you all together as a team. We think it's important. So, this is the plan. Since you all want to reside on Bear Island we have come up with a solution. Dana and Marilyn, you will guide all of the other teams. Your job is to train the recruits we send you," Sam says as he waits for a response.

"Okay, I like that idea. But where is there room on Bear Island to do that? The island is already covered with Bear Island Camp buildings and cabins. Is there room for a training camp too?" Dana asks.

Marilyn looks to Sam for an answer and says, "Will they need to be trained off site?"

"I knew I picked the right two to work on this. Yes, they will be trained on a nearby island. When we purchased Bear Island, we also bought a bigger nearby island. We knew if our operation was successful, we would need more space. Bear Island has been very successful, and we also need to think ahead twenty years when those children have their own families. Will they choose to stay on Bear Island or leave? Many of them will decide to stay and we need to have homes for them. Dana, Marilyn you two will be training the people we send you. Much like the training Joy did for you," Sam says.

There is a silence and we look at each other. It's been such a short time since Joy left but we have had so many changes since then.

"Do you two think you are up for the challenge? You will have a permanent residence on Bear Island, but also a cabin on the training site. Transportation to and from your work site will be by boat."

At that moment Dana says, "We have to go by boat? How cool! I'm in. How about you Marilyn?"

"Yes, I'm in. It sounds intriguing," she says.

Marcos and I are nervous. We have no idea what Sam has in mind for us. We know he'll keep us on Bear Island but not sure in what capacity.

"Okay, Marcos and Margarita we have a project you may like. I'm going you let you two decide which one of you takes the two jobs we have in mind. We want you to choose."

"Okay, what are the two jobs?" I ask.

"Okay two positions. Bear Island Camp Commander. Think about the title for a moment."

Mary Ellen says, "What do you think the Bear Island Camp Commander would do?"

I speak up first, "Keep everything organized and under control on Bear Island?"

Marcos says, "Train staff and make sure kids are safe and placed in right families?"

"You both are right. Plus, a lot of other activities. Are either of you interested in that position?"

We both raise our hands. Will they have to choose one of us to be in charge of the whole island? I think to myself.

"Would you choose that job without knowing what the other job is?" Sam asks.

Now I wonder what the other job could be. Maybe Assistant to the Commander?

"I am interested in that job," Marcos says. "But if Margarita wants it, I can do the other job."

I look at Marcos and I don't know what to do. They are offering one of us a wonderful job. I can't take that opportunity away from Marcos. I decide to tell Sam.

"I think Marcos would do a great job as Commander of Bear Island Camp. I think it should be his job," I say.

"What if he prefers the other job?" Sam asks.

"Can we find out what the other one is first? Is it assistant to the commander?" I ask.

"No, it's not an assistant job. It's another commander job," Sam says.

Silence envelopes the room. Another commander job? What could it be?

"I agree with you both, I think Marcos would make a great Commander of Bear Island Camp. Either one of you really, but Marcos may enjoy that job more than the other."

"Can you tell us what the other one is?" I ask.

"Sure, but first I want to give you a little background. Bear Island Camp was formed out of the need to provide those kids with a safe place to grow and thrive. They weren't given a good start, the fact they were born into poverty in a country that has few opportunities for them except to go North to work is troubling. You couple that with what happened to them at the border and it is a total case of family separation and most of all child abuse. We couldn't sit by and watch while that happened if we had the money and staff to help out. Bear Island Camp is the result. Now the next stage is to plan for their futures.

We have staff here working on the search for their families. As you know we have only been able to re-home very few. You know the numbers because you helped fly them to San Diego.

While the staff continues to search for the families, we also have to plan for the realistic view that we may never be able to find them. That is one of the reasons they are on Bear Island.

Mary Ellen and I also have other projects. This is one of many. We have other goals as well as the child rescue from the border. We now know there are other centers around the United States where the children have been relocated. We have a group working on a plan for those centers. The need is endless. We need to turn some of our projects over to someone else. I think you or Marcos could be the person to fill that position."

"Which position? I don't follow," I say.

"Commander of Field Operations, the person in that position would be in charge of organizing all of the rescue missions, including flights, payments, staffing and follow up with all of the staff involved. The position would be based on Bear Island. You two will be moving to a new home. In the home you will have a control center like we have here with computers, information databases and a budget to run it all. A staff would relocate from here to work with you. You will be supervising a staff of ten, plus interface with Dana and Marilyn with their trainings. They will get all of their information through you. In essence, none of you will be working with us. You will be a self-contained operation. Of course, I will be here if you need help with anything. What do you think?"

Marcos speaks first, "I think you have just described the perfect job for Margarita. She is definitely the one better suited for that job. I am interested in the Bear Island job."

I look over at Marcos. What did he just say? Did he say he wants me to take the Field Operations Commander job? I'm interested in both, but I am intrigued by the Field Operations job.

"Well, Sam you know the baby is due in January. How will that work? I can work while I'm pregnant, but I need some time off when the baby comes. Especially if I take either commander job," I say.

"We have that all planned out. We'd like you to start training now. You can finish the term online. We'll do some training here before you move to Bear Island. The majority of your training will be on-the job. Mary Ellen and I will still be in charge until you decide you are ready to take over. It could be six months or up to a year. You decide. You'll have excellent day care available."

"I can take that much time off?" I ask.

"Of course, you will be living on Bear Island anyway. You can decide to work or not work. The training will be ongoing, so it may involve a few hours a day if you want to come back to work on a part time basis," Sam says.

"Marcos, what do you think? Do you want to move to Bear Island and work there?" I ask.

"I think it will be the best place for us to raise the baby and I know you'll make a great commander of field operations," Marcos says.

"Are you sure? I think you'd make a great commander too, but I would prefer the Field Operations if you don't mind," I say.

"I never doubted you would want it any other way," Marcos says.

"Dana and Marilyn, are you happy with going to Bear Island too? I wouldn't want to leave my friends behind. Are you interested in the position as Training Coordinators?" I ask.

Dana answers first, "What do you think? I get to take a boat to work every day. It sounds perfect."

Marilyn smiles and says, "Once we have the wedding on Bear Island, why would we leave? I love the idea of working with you all. You are my family now. I'm not giving up the chance to live on an island surrounded by all of the people I love the most. I can't wait!"

Sam looks at us all and smiles. "This is by far my favorite team! I didn't have a plan if any of you decided not to move to Bear Island. All of you had to be involved in order for it to work."

Tears stream down my face and I remember what it took for us to get to this point. I started out alone with

Tía Elena in San Felipe. Then the long trip to Oregon to live with Tío Enrique. That all happened before I met Marcos. Our work at Fish Camp on the Sea Breeze brought us close together. Yasmene and Miguel were our friends there too. We were moved from the Sea Breeze to a smaller ship, I thought it was to go work in Alaska, but it had been arranged so I could reunite with my family. What a surprise that was for me. I thought my family had been killed in a car accident. To find out they were there waiting for me was such a relief. Our relocation with WITSEC helped us escape from my Tío Enrique and his associates. We were relocated twice with our final location being Oswego.

So many things could have gone wrong. So many times, we could have been separated, but to think now we will all be living on Bear Island together is the perfect ending to a sad story. What started as my journey to freedom led to me landing on an island off the coast of Nova Scotia with my entire family. The arrival of our baby will make it perfect. I think we should name her Esperanza; hope was what got us all here together, and she will help us start our next chapter in our lives.

Bear Island Camp

ABOUT THE AUTHOR

Kate Banco, an Indie Author, lives in in the Pacific Northwest.

This is her third novel in the series.

Fish Camp, A Young Girl's Journey to Freedom

Forensics Camp, Where there is always an Unbelievable Story

Bear Island Camp, A Place to Call Home

Contact Kate Banco: KateBancoAuthor@gmail.com

Join Kate Banco Readers on Facebook

Twitter:@KateBancoauthor

www.katebancoauthor.wixsite.com/KateBanco

Kate appreciates all reviews on amazon.com, goodreads.com and bookbub.com

Made in the USA
Coppell, TX
22 December 2020

45245384R00118